"FOR SCIENCE-FICTION FANS, DONALD A. WOLLHEIM'S THE SECRET OF THE NINTH PLANET WILL PROVIDE PLENTY OF EXCITEMENT." —*El Paso Times*

"A secret installation in the Andes stealing the world's supply of sun heat is the starting point for an exciting voyage of adventure, taking a picked crew of Terran scientists through our solar system to trace down and destroy a threat against the human planet.

"The vivid descriptions of the contrasting conditions on the various worlds and moons, as the Terran ship fights an unseen, unknown enemy, are excellently done."

—*Cleveland Press*

"SUSPENSEFUL."

—*Book List*

"A LIVELY TALE."

—*Windsor Star*

"AN AMAZING THEME . . . A REAL THRILLER."

—*Ft. Worth Star*

THE SECRET
OF THE
NINTH PLANET

Donald A. Wollheim

PAPERBACK LIBRARY, Inc.
New York

PAPERBACK LIBRARY EDITION

First Printing: November, 1965

For—
Three denizens of this minor planet:
Eleanor, Bill and of course Janet.

Copyright © 1959 by Donald A. Wollheim

Library of Congress Catalog Card Number: 59-5328

This Paperback Library Edition is published
by arrangement with Holt, Rinehart and Winston.

Paperback Library books are published by Paperback Library, Inc. Its
trademark, consisting of the words "Paperback Library" and associated
distinctive design, is registered in the United States Patent Office.
Paperback Library, Inc., 260 Park Avenue South, New York, N.Y. 10010.

Covers Printed in U.S.A.
Body Text Printed in Canada.

WHILE THE circumnavigation of the solar system seems farfetched, it may not be once the problem of effective anti-gravitational control is solved. In this book I have assumed that the many researchers now actually at work on this problem will achieve such a result in the next decade. It is not at all impossible that they may—for we all know that the more minds that work at a problem, the sooner it will be solved. The discovery of a means of negating, reversing or otherwise utilizing the immense force of gravitation for space flight purposes is now thought to be within the bounds of probability. It should occur some time within the next hundred years, possibly in even the short period I assume here.

Once solved, the severe handicaps imposed on space exploration by the weight and chemical limitations of rockets would no longer apply. The whole timetable of our conquest of the planets in our solar system would be tremendously speeded up, from hot Mercury all the way out to frigid Pluto.

In describing the visits of the spaceship *Magellan* to the planets, I have endeavored to adhere to known facts and the more reasonable assumptions about each of these worlds. The planet Pluto, however, deserves further comment, occupying as it does both an important role in this adventure and a unique one in actual astronomical lore.

Back at the dawn of this century, many astronomers, and notably Dr. Percival Lowell, studied certain irregularities in the orbit and motion of Neptune, at that time believed to be the outermost planet. They decided that these eccentricities (or perturbations, as they are called) could only be caused by the presence of another, yet undiscovered planet beyond Neptune.

Following this line of research, a young astronomer, Dr. Clyde Tombaugh, working at Lowell's own observatory, was able to announce on March 13, 1930, that he had finally found this ninth world, which he named Pluto.

In the years that have followed, Pluto has proven to be a truly puzzling planet. Unlike its neighbors from Jupiter outward, it is not a giant world, light and gaseous in nature. Instead, it belongs physically to the small, dense inner planets of which Earth is one.

The latest viewpoint on this planet, whose size and weight seem quite like those of Earth, is that it may not be a true child of the Sun, but an outsider captured as it roamed the trackless realms of galactic space. Its orbit is highly eccentric and rather lopsided, taking it as far away from the Sun as four and a half billion miles and as close to the Sun as two and three-quarter billion miles, thereby cutting inside the orbit of Neptune itself. In fact, during the period from 1969 to 2009 (covering most of the lifetimes of the younger readers of this book) Pluto will not be the ninth planet, but the eighth, for it will be at its closest in those years. Huge Neptune will thus regain temporarily the title of being the Sun's farthest outpost!

This orbital eccentricity has lead some astronomers to speculate on the possibility that Pluto may once have been briefly held as a satellite of Neptune. And following that line of thought, the possibility also has been suggested that Neptune's larger moon, Triton, may once have been a companion of Pluto which failed to break away from Neptune's grip!

I think that the first men to land on Pluto are going to make some very astonishing discoveries. But I am also sure that they will never go there in rockets. They will have to make the immense trip by some more powerful means—like the anti-gravitational drive.

D.A.W.

CHAPTER ONE

Special Delivery—by Guided Missile

ON THE morning that the theft of the solar system's sunlight began, Burl Denning woke up in his sleeping bag in the Andes, feeling again the exhilaration of the keen, rarefied, mountain air. He glanced at the still sleeping forms of his father and the other members of the Denning expedition, and sat up, enjoying the first rays of the early morning.

The Llamas were already awake, moving restlessly back and forth on their padded feet, waiting for their tender to arise and unleash them. The mules were standing patiently as ever, staring quietly into the distant misty panorama of the mountains.

It was, thought Burl, a dim day, but this he supposed was due to the earliness of the morning. As the Sun rose, it would rapidly bring the temperatures up, and its unshielded rays would force them to cover up as they climbed along the high mountain passes.

The sky was cloudless as usual. Burl assumed that the dimness was due to volcanic dust, or some unseen high cloud far away. And, indeed, as the expedition came to life, and the day began in earnest, nobody paid any attention to the fact that the Sun was not quite so warm as it should have been.

The Denning expedition, questing among the untracked and forgotten byways of the lost Inca ruins in the vast, jagged mountains of inland Peru, was not alone in failing to notice the subtle channeling away of the Sun's warmth and brilliance. They were, in this respect, one with virtually the entire population of Earth.

In New York, in San Francisco, in Philadelphia and Kansas City, people going about their day's chores simply assumed that there must be clouds somewhere —the temperature only slightly less than normal for a

July day. A few men shaded their eyes and looked about, noticing that the heat was not too intense—and thought it a blessing.

In some places in Europe, there were clouds and a little rain, and the dimness was ascribed to this. It was raining in much of Asia, and there were scattered afternoon showers throughout Latin America, which were standard for the season. There was a flurry of snow in Melbourne and a cold blow in Santiago de Chile.

The men in the weather bureaus noted on their day's charts that temperatures were a few degress lower than had been predicted, but that was nothing unusual. Weather was still not entirely predictable, even with the advances of meteorology that were to be expected of the latter years of the twentieth century.

The world was reading about other things than the vagaries of the weather. In the United States, baseball occupied the headlines, and the nonathletic-minded could find some speculative interest in the completion of another manned space platform racing along in its eternal orbit twelve thousand miles away from Earth's surface. The U.S. Moon Base in the center of the Crater Ptolemaeus had described the appearance of this platform in an interesting radio dispatch which appeared on the first pages of most newspapers. The third prober rocket sent to Venus had been unreported for the tenth day after penetrating the clouds that hid that planet's surface from human eyes. It was, like its two predecessors, a minimum-sized, unmanned instrument device designed to penterate the clouds and radio back data on the nature of the Venusian atmosphere and the surface. But after its first report, nothing more had been heard.

Some discussion was going on in science circles about what had happened. Speculation centered on the possible success of other types of prober rockets, but it was universally agreed that the time had not come when a manned rocket could safely undertake the difficult trip to Venus and return.

The years of space flight since the orbiting of Sputnik I back in 1957 had produced many fascinating results, but they had also brought a realization of the many problems that surrounded the use of rockets for space flight. It was generally believed that no one should risk a manned flight until absolutely everything possible that could be learned by robot and radio-controlled missiles had been learned. It now looked as if Venus and Mars trips were still a dozen years away.

Burl Denning was keenly interested in all of this. As a senior in high school, the newly expanding frontiers of the universe represented something special to his generation. It would be men of his own age who would eventually man those first full-scale expeditions to neighbor worlds. By the time he was out of college, with an engineering degree, he might himself hope to be among those adventurers of space.

Burl was torn between two interests. Archaeology was both a profession and a hobby in the Denning family. His grandfather had been among the first to explore the jungle ruins of Indochina. His father, although a businessman and industrial engineer, made annual vacation pilgrimages to the ruins of the old Indian civilizations of the Americas. Burl had been with him once before, when they had trekked through the chicle forests of Guatemala in search of a lost Mayan city. And now they were again on a quest, this time for the long-forgotten treasure of the Incas.

Burl was thoroughly familiar with the techniques of tracking down the ancient records of mankind. He got along well with natives and primitive people; he knew the arts of wilderness survival; he knew the delicate techniques of sifting sand and dirt to turn up those priceless bits of pottery and chipped stone that could supply pages of the forgotten epics of human history.

However, later in the day it seemed as if their particular camp had petered out. There were ruins there—a broken-down wall, a dry well and a bit of eroded basrelief lying on its side. Burl's father looked at him thoughtfully. The tall, sandy-haired youth was sitting astraddle a pile of dust, methodically sifting it through a wide-mesh strainer. A large pile of sifted sand gave evidence of the length of his efforts, and one broken bit of clay was the only result he had obtained.

Two of the Indian guides sat patiently in the shade, watching them. One was digging slowly, turning up more dirt to be sifted.

"I think we've had enough here," said the elder Denning. "Burl, you can knock off. Tomorrow we'll pull up stakes and see what is in the next valley. We'll try to follow that old Inca road over the mountains. I don't believe anyone has ever penetrated there—and the airplane surveys indicated some evidence of human dwellings."

Burl nodded, and set the sifter down. He'd learned to curb his natural energies for the exacting tasks required of serious scientific research. "Okay," he said, "I was hoping you'd move on soon, Dad. This looked like a washout from the first. I'd say this place was sacked and ruined even before the Incas fell."

The older man nodded. "I suppose so. Well, let's wash up and see what's for supper."

They went down to the icy mountain stream to wash the dirt from their hands. "It's been a nice day," Burl commented. "In spite of the Sun being out steadily, it wasn't hot at all. Cooler than yesterday."

Mark Denning looked up at the sky and the Sun lowering toward the horizon. "There must have been some volcanic dust in the heavens," he said. "The Sun's been a bit dimmed, have you noticed?"

Burl squinted his eyes against the glare. "Wasn't any eruption around here. Maybe in Ecuador?"

His father shrugged. "Could have been thousands of miles away," was his slow reply. "Volcanic dust travels around the world, just as radioactive dust permeated the atmosphere from atomic testings. They say that the dust from the great Krakatoa explosion remained in the atmosphere for three years before the last of it settled."

When they had finished supper and the Sun was casting its last red rays over the rapidly purpling landscape, Burl got out the expedition radio, set up its antenna, plugged in its compact atomic battery, and tried to get the news from Lima. All he got was static.

He fiddled with the dials for a long time, twisting the antenna, ranging the wavelengths, but there was static everywhere. "Strange," he said to his father, "something's disturbed reception completely."

Pedro Gonzales, their official Peruvian guide, leaned over. "Could be the battery she is broken, eh?"

Burl shook his head. "Not this battery," he said. "It's a brand-new one, a real keen development. And I already checked the wiring. It's some sort of disturbance that's blocking reception. Maybe we're in a dead zone or something."

"Wasn't dead yesterday," said his father. "Maybe that eruption was radioactive."

Burl looked up sharply. "I'll check the Geiger counters, Dad. Something's blocking reception, something strong and powerful to interfere with this set." But when he returned, he had to admit he had found nothing.

When the Sun went down, they retired, for the temperature drops swiftly in the high, thin air of the Andes.

In the rest of the world people watched their color-vision shows without interruption. Reception was good with the Moon base, the space platforms had no difficulty making reports, and the radio news beamed out as usual. In Lima, there was a little static, and direct transmission with Brazil seemed partially disrupted, but that was all.

In the following five days, the Denning expedition had managed the difficult climb over the next range of mountains and had come down in the high plateau valley between. In this same period, the world began to realize that the dimness of the sky was not a temporary phenomenon.

Weather stations noted that the past few days had all been several degrees under the average. Reports had come in that farmers were querying the unusual drop in the temperatures at night. And astronomers, measuring the surface heat of the Sun, came up with strange discrepancies from previous data.

One astronomer communicated with another, and a general exchange of advice began. In a short while, a communication was laid on the desk of the President of the United States, who scanned it and had it immediately transmitted to the Secretary General of the United Nations. The Secretary General circulated the report among the scientific bureaus of all member nations, and this led in turn to a meeting of the Security Council. This meeting was held in quiet, without benefit of newspaper reporters or audience.

There was no longer any doubt. The radiation of the Sun reaching the face of the Earth had decreased. The facts were indisputable. Where a day should have registered, in some places, at least 90° in the Sun, a reading of only 84° was noted. Measurements definitely showed that the face of the Sun visible to man on Earth had dimmed by just that margin.

This might not prove serious at first, but as the scientists called in by the Security Council pointed out, it promised terrible things as the year went on. A difference of five or ten degress all over the Earth could mean the ruin of certain crops, it could mean an increase in snowfall and frost that could very rapidly destroy the economies and habitability of many places on the Earth's teeming surface.

"But what," asked the Chairman of the Council, "is causing this decrease in solar energy?"

This the astronomers could not answer. But they pointed to one factor. The reports from the U.S. Moon Base did not agree with the observations from Earth. Moon instruments claimed no decrease whatsoever in the amount of sunlight reaching the arid, airless surface of the Earth's only satellite.

The cause was somewhere on Earth. And the Security Council requested the careful scanning of the Earth from space platforms and the Moon to determine the center of the trouble.

Burl Denning had not found the next valley of much

interest, either. Evidence of an Inca road over the mountain had petered out. There were signs there had been human dwellings, but they were not Inca—just reminders of the onetime passage of an unknown band of primitives who had grazed their sheep, built temporary tents, and pulled up stakes perhaps a hundred years before.

So again at night, Burl, his father, and Gonzales took counsel. They were debating which way to proceed next; Mark Denning reasoning that they should go further inland, following tales natives had told; Gonzales urging that they retrack their path and proceed northward toward the regions where Inca ruins abounded.

For the past week Burl had not been able to get radio reception. The static had increased as they had gone eastward over the mountain, but not a word of news or any human voiee came through. The Moon was rising on the horizon as Burl sat playing with the antenna. Finally he gave up and switched it off.

The discussion had died away and the three men were quiet. The Indian guides had retired to their own campfire, and one of them had taken out his pipes and was blowing a soft, plaintive tune.

Burl stared at the full Moon in silence, wondering if he would ever have a chance to walk its surface, or if his own future was to lie in probing mankind's past rather than surveying the grounds of his future. As he watched, he thought he saw a faint light among the brightening stars where none had been before.

He squinted, and, sure enough, he saw that one tiny white light was swinging more and more toward the center of the sky. He pointed it out to his father and Gonzales. "Too fast to be a celestial object," he said. "Is it one of the space platforms or a sputnik?"

The two men gazed at it in curiosity. Suddenly it seemed to grow brighter and sharper and to twist toward them in its path.

"Look!" gasped Burl, but the others were already on their feet.

The light plunged down. There was a sudden outburst of yellow flame that caused the three to duck instinctively, and brought the Indians to their feet with yells. The glare brightened until they could see that something was just above them. The fire vanished as swiftly as it came, but a white spot of light remained.

"It's a parachute!" Burl shouted. "It's a rocket or something, braking to a stop above us, and coming down by parachute!"

In the pale light of the full Moon they saw that something metallic and glistening hung from the white mushroom of a parachute. There was a clanging sound as it hit the rocky earth with a soft, sighing whoosh. The cloth of the parachute settled.

They ran across the dry stone of the valley floor, but Burl's long, athletic legs outdistanced the others. He reached it first.

It was a cylinder of metal, about three feet long and a foot in diameter.

"It's the nose of a message missile—dropped from a guided missile," Burl announced. "And—look!" He dramatically pointed the beam of his flashlight upon its side.

There, written in black, heat-resistant paint, were the words: *To the Denning Andes Expedition, from U.S. Air Force Base, California Region. By Guided Missile Post by Moon Base control, Ptolomaeus Crater. Official. Open Without Delay.*

CHAPTER TWO

The Valley of Stolen Sunlight

FOR A moment all three were silent with amazement. "From California—and Moon Base—for *us?*" gasped Burl, finally. "But why? What can they want of us?"

His father frowned. "Only way to find out is to open it and see." He squatted down to study the cylinder closer. Burl pointed a finger at the nose.

"Looks like a crack there. Maybe it unscrews. Let's lift it."

It was not as heavy as it had appeared, for, like all rocket missiles, it was made of the light but tough alloys that were necessary to conserve weight-lift costs and fuel reserves. They stood it upright and tried to turn the top. After a little resistance, it unscrewed slowly. Inside, they found a rolled document bearing the seal of the United States Air Force.

Burl took it out, and unfolded it with unsteady hands. His father read over his shoulder.

Gonzales poked at the empty cylinder, impatiently. Finally, he burst out, "What does it say? What do they want?"

Burl turned to him. "It's unbelievable! It's—it's just so darned surprising! The dimness of the days, the drop in temperature—it wasn't just around here! It was all over the world!"

Quickly, he went on to tell the Peruvian what they had just learned. The communication was from the U.S. Space Commission and it had been directed on its flight from California by the Moon Base, because only from the satellite could the exact location of the Dennings be spotted. It seemed that the Dennings were the only scientifically trained personnel close to the point on Earth where the disturbance originated. This also accounted for the blanketing of radio waves in their vicinity. Several airplanes had tried to locate them, but strange disturbances in the ether and atmosphere had made it impossible to establish contact. Also, the back reaches of the Andes were poorly mapped and treacherous in air currents, even in normal times.

"During the last week, a certain fraction of the Sun's light and energy reaching the Earth has been diverted. It has been bent or focused in much the same way that a lens bends light rays—and the point to which it has been directed is a spot only seven miles from here! Over that last mountain range," said Burl, pointing.

Gonzales followed his finger. "Just over the mountains lies the source of the trouble," said Burl excitedly. "And we're the nearest to it. They want us to go over there, see what it is, stop it, or report back. It took the telescopes in Moon Base to locate us and to track the center of the trouble!"

Mark Denning pursed his lips. "We'll have to start tomorrow, and we'll have to go fast. A loss of light and heat, however slight, could have very serious effects on life if continued too long. We can make it by tomorrow night, if we start early and leave the Indians and pack animals behind."

The other two nodded. Mark looked at them in the half-light of the Moon. "You'll have to stay with the equipment, Pedro, otherwise the Indians might abandon it. Burl and I will start out at dawn."

Gonzales agreed and the three made their way back to the camp. At the first sign of light breaking in the morning horizon, Burl and his father started off. They carried only enough equipment for survival, plus the additional items that might be needed for the emergency ahead.

The trek over the mountains was a hard one, the path narrow, steep, sometimes nonexistent. There were few signs of Indians or animals, and it was plain that few ever traveled over this range. The air was cold and thin, vegetation sparse and hardy. All around them was the cold blue of the sky—a shade darker than usual—and the gaunt peaks of ancient mountains. The Inca

16

kings may have claimed the land here, but even their hardy legions had never conquered these lonely and hostile sky domains.

Panting and weary with hours of climbing, Burl and his father made a quick lunch in a sheltered jumble of rock near the top. Then, shouldering their packs again, they trudged on. At last they reached a point where the view of the other side spread out before them—a breathtakingly clear vision of the little valley below.

As they looked down, the air seemed to shimmer and vibrate. Burl rubbed his eyes. "It hurts," he said.

His father squinted. "There's a powerful vibrational effect. It may be a very dangerous concentration of the invisible rays of the Sun as well as of light."

Once Burl had gotten used to the odd visual effect, which was like gazing into the twisting heat rays rising from an overheated oven, he saw that there was a small flat region between the mountains. And in the center of this valley was a large black structure of some sort. The twisting effect of the light around it made it impossible to tell more.

"That's it," said Burl. His father nodded, shifted the pack to ease his shoulders, unstrapped the hunting rifle slung over his back, and carefully checked its loads.

Burl saw what his father was doing and suddenly understood the danger. What could be doing a thing like this? What but something not of this Earth? Something of distant space, of a science beyond that of man —and *unfriendly* besides. Now, for the first time, Burl realized what he had not had time to before—this was an enemy he and his father were facing—an enemy of all mankind—and utterly unknown.

He gulped, gripped his rifle, and followed his father down the sliding rocky trail.

As they drew nearer the base of the mountain, the effects of the strange vibrations grew more pronounced. Burl avoided looking directly ahead, keeping his eyes on the ground before his feet, yet even so, he could not help noticing how the stones around them seemed to shimmer in the invisible waves. From the base of the

17

valley the sky now seemed streaked with black and gray rings, as if they were reaching the center of some atmospheric whirlpool. Out of the mountains, after hours of arduous scrambling, they started across the barren rocky plain.

Before them rose a vast circular structure several stories high, ominously black and without any sign of windows or doors. Above the building protruded two great projections ending in huge, shining discs. One of the monstrous cuplike discs was facing the Sun, the other pointed in the opposite direction.

As the two men came nearer and nearer, the strangeness in the air increased. They felt they were being penetrated through and through with invisible lances, with tiny prickles of heat. "Radiation?" queried Burl softly, afraid of the answer. His father trudged grimly on for a moment, and then put down his pack. He took out a Geiger counter and activated it.

He shook his head. "No radioactivity," he said. "Whatever this is, it isn't that."

They reached the wall of the building. Oddly, here they seemed sheltered from the unusual vibrations. Burl realized that the source was above them, probably the two mighty discs raised high in the sky.

The Dennings surveyed the building, but found no entrance. It must have been a quarter of a mile around its walls, but there was no sign of a door or entry. The wall was of a rocklike substance, but it was not like any rock or plastic Burl had ever seen.

"We've got to get in," said Burl as they returned to the starting point, "but how?"

His father smiled. "This way." He opened his pack and took two cans of blasting powder from it. "I thought these would come in handy. Lucky we had some left over from the blasting we did last week."

He set both cans at the base of the high wall, wired them together, and ran the wire as far as it reached. When the two men were a safe distance away, Mark sparked off the explosive.

There was a thunderous roar: rocks and dirt showered around them, and bits of black powdery stuff. When the smoke cleared, Burl and his father leaped to their feet, rifles in hand.

There was a crack in the side of the wall where the explosive had gone off. And the rip was large enough to get through!

Without a word, they charged across the ground, still smoking from the concussion, and squeezed through the mysterious walls of the enigmatic building.

The walls were thin, thin but hard, as befit masters of atomic engineering. Inside, they found a roomless building—one single chamber within the frame of the outer walls.

A dim, bluish light emanated from the curving ceiling. On the uncleared rocky ground which was the floor of the building were a number of huge machines.

They were spherical glassy inventions, many times the height of a man, connected by strings of thick metal bars and rows of smaller globes, none of which was familiar. There was a steady humming noise, and above, the two giant, metal masts penetrating the ceiling rotated slowly. Doubtless, the great Sun-trapping discs were affixed to the top of these masts.

There was no living thing in sight.

Burl and his father stood silently, half crouched, with rifles at the ready, but nothing moved to challenge them. There was only the humming of the Sun transmitters.

Burl called out, but there was no answer. They advanced cautiously, fearing a trap. The place did not have the look of living things about it. "An automatic station," said Mark under his breath. "I think it's strictly automatic."

It gradually became evident that Mark was right. Everything was automatic. Whoever had built this structure to divert the rays of the Sun had simply set it down, put it in motion, and left. There was no evidence of any provisions for a garrison or a director.

They studied the machines but could make nothing of them. They found what looked like controls, but although they pushed and pulled the levers and knobs, the humming did not cease. It seemed as if the controls were either dummies or had to be specially motivated.

"What do we do now?" asked Burl, after they had tried pulling all the levers on one particular switchboard without any results. "Do you have enough powder left to blow up the machinery?"

His father shook his head. "I had only those two cans with me. We could try shooting into the machinery." Leveling his rifle, he fired at a glassy globe perched upon the central sphere. The bullet pinged off it, and they saw that it had failed even to dent the glistening surface.

"It won't work," said the elder Denning, after several more shots had produced the same result and the concussion reverberating from the enclosed walls had nearly deafened them.

They continued to hunt for a clue, but found none. Dejected, Burl kicked a loose pebble and watched it rattle against a column near the main control board. A small metallic ball rested on top of the column, apparently unattached. A replacement part, he thought to himself, wandering over to it. It was about the level of his head.

With the thought that if he examined it he might learn something of the nature of the working machines, he reached out with both hands to pick it up.

As his hands touched the metallic ball, there was a sudden terrible flash of power. He felt himself grasped by forces beyond his control, paralyzed momentarily like one who has laid hold of an electrically charged wire. He opened his mouth to scream in agony, but he could say nothing. A great force surged through his body, radiating, charging every cell and atom of his being. He felt as if he were being lifted from the floor. Then the globe seemed to dissolve in his hands. It became a glare of light, grew misty, and then vanished.

For a moment he stood there on tiptoe, arced with the potent violence of the force, glowing from within with energies, and then he felt as if the supercharge were dissolving itself, slipping into him, sliding into the ground, then disappearing.

He stood before the column, swaying, but still conscious and alive. His hands were still raised, but there was no ball between them, neither of metal nor of power.

He let them fall to his side and took a step. He was whole, he was sound, he was unharmed. He heard his father's footsteps running to him, and murmured weakly, "I'm all right."

And he was. He could see no sign of damage. "I must have absorbed an awful lot of that energy—or whatever it was," he said.

After resting a moment, he decided to try the useless controls again. Going over to one small board, he idly shoved a lever. This time he felt resistance. The lever was activated. There was a slight change in the radiance of one globe.

"Dad!" Burl shouted. "It works! It works for me now!"

Mark Denning watched as Burl turned dials and levers and got responses. "You must have been charged in a special way," he said excitedly. "That's how they lock their devices. They will only respond to a person carrying that special energy charge, whatever it was. Come on, let's get to the main control, before the effect goes away—if it does."

The two dashed to the panel which, they guessed, activated the main Sun transmitter. Burl grabbed the instruments and threw them back to what seemed to be the zero positions.

The humming rose in intensity, then quieted down and finally stopped. There was a series of clicks, and one by one, the various globes, condensers and glowing machines died out. Above them came a whirring noise, and Burl looked up to see the masts withdrawing into the building, their discs presumably left flat and directionless.

It felt different. Suddenly they knew that the vibrations which had been so heavy in the air about them were gone. There was silence everywhere, the natural silence of an empty, lifeless building in an uninhabited valley.

Burl and his father made their way to the break in the wall and climbed through it.

Outside, the Sun shone down brighter than it had before. The sky was the calm serene blue of a cloudless day. Burl knew that at that same moment, all over the world, the sky was clearer and the Sun warmer.

But for how long? Behind them the building still stood—and its inventors were still to be found.

CHAPTER THREE

The Secret of A-G 17

THE DENNINGS did not have much time to speculate on the mystery of the Sun-stealers. For just as they were discussing what should be their next course of action, the problem was solved for them. There was a roaring in the air, then a humming, and in a matter of a few more seconds, six rocket helicopters popped into sight, hovered over the valley on streaming jets, and settled down.

"They're U.S. planes!" gasped Burl, jumping to his feet and going to meet them. "It must mean that they know we stopped the machines."

"Obviously," said his father, striding with him to greet the helmeted man who was now stepping out of the lead machine. By this time the last of the squad had landed, and the khaki-clad soldiers in them were already disembarking. "I imagine that all over the world the sky turned a little brighter. It must have been apparent at once."

The leader of the 'copter men reached them. He was a tall, bronzed man, wearing the service coveralls and markings of a captain of the Air Force. He stretched out his hand. "You must be the Dennings. I'm Captain Saunders. I've been asked to bring you back with me right away so that we can get a complete report on this affair. How fast can you get ready?"

"Why," said Burl, "we're ready right now. As soon as we can dump our packs aboard. But, gee, you mean go back—where?"

Saunders smiled grimly. "To California. We just left there. I have been given urgent orders to waste no time. So will you oblige?"

The two Dennings looked at each other. This was important, all right. They realized that these planes had flown on fast rockets the instant the sky had cleared. Possibly there was still a crisis—one they had not heard of.

They did not pause to ask further questions. Mark Denning asked the captain to dispatch one of his 'copters to the camp beyond the mountains to tell Gonzales to load up and start back for Lima. This order given, the two Dennings climbed into the rocket 'copter, and Saunders took the controls.

With a whoosh, the squat craft lifted on its rockets, its jet-driven fan carried it up, folded, and the rocket engine took over. On upward into the stratosphere they hurtled, across the Western Hemisphere, across the face of jungle and isthmus, across the barren mountains of Mexico, and in a matter of less than half an hour, settled down in the wide open field of a U.S. Air Force base in southern California. It was all so swift, so sudden, that to Burl it seemed like a dream. There had been so many days in the field, in the peace and quiet of the high mountains of the Andes. There had been the slow hunting around age-worn ruins; the careful, deliberate sifting of tons of soil and sand for tiny shards; then this: the urgent message, the trek, the weird building, the strange, body-filling shock, and the control over the Sun-theft globes, followed by the swift transition over thousands of miles.

Here he was in his home country—weeks sooner than he had expected—but not to return to his home and school. No, for he felt that somehow an adventure was beginning that could lead anywhere. Perhaps his adventure had actually ended, but he saw now that he would be questioned, probed, and asked to recount his story over and over.

Burl and his father were met at the port by a group of officers and escorted rapidly to a room in a large building. Here there were half a dozen men in civilian clothes. One by one, these men were introduced, and as each one was named, Burl wondered more about what was to come.

There was a general from Army Intelligence. There

was a high member of the State Department. There were three noted astronomers—among them the surprisingly young Russell Clyde and the elderly and famous Dr. Merckmann. There was an aircraft manufacturer whose name graced a thousand planes, and an engineer who had contributed to the conquest of the Moon.

The general, Walton Shrove, asked them to sit down. He was in charge of the affair. It turned out to be a careful questioning of their story. It was not a hounding of questions as in a police quizzing, or a baiting from newspapermen eager to get a scoop. Rather, their questions were deliberate and intelligent. They drew out the full account of what Burl and his father had seen in that valley, and of what the Sun-theft globes appeared to be like in operation. They concentrated deeply on the curious experience which had placed in Burl the charge that enabled him to control the machines.

"Would you mind," the general asked Burl, "if we subject you to a series of medical and electronic tests to determine whether this charge is still with you?"

Burl shook his head. "I'll go along with anything you say."

"Very well," the general smiled. "We'll make our purposes clear to you afterward. But we want to get this over as soon as we can."

Burl left the room in company with three technicians who had come in. They took him to the medical office at the base and there he was given a complete check. At the electronics lab, electrodes were attached to him and careful readings were made of the natural electrical resistance of his body, and of his apparent physical charge. After an hour of tests, Burl was brought back to the main council room.

As he entered, he sensed he had interrupted something important. His father looked at him, and Burl detected in his face a certain curious mingling of pride and parental concern. What, the young man wondered, were they up to?

25

When he was seated, the company grew silent. The general pursed his lips, looked directly at Burl, and said, "I think the time has come to acquaint you with the problem our world is facing. We may ask you to make a very personal decision, and we think you ought to know what may hang on it."

He stopped. Every face at the table was grim. Mark Denning, too, was sober, though Burl detected that he also did not quite know what was to come.

"It is apparent that some race of beings, some species from outer space, unknown to us, has begun a process of tapping the power and light of the Sun for transmission elsewhere. The station on Earth, which you shut down, was an important one. But . . . it was not the only one. There are others, operating in this solar system." He nodded to Merckmann.

The old astronomer took the cue. "The observatories of the Earth, aided by the lunar observers, have definitely determined that there is still a certain amount of light being shifted from the faces of other planets and diverted. We have detected by telescopic and telethermic measurements that there are areas of Sun-disturbances on the surfaces of the planets Mercury and Mars. We suspect the existence of one on Venus. We believe that this may prove to be true on other planets as well, but we have no doubt of the first two.

"Measurements of the amount of Sun power being piped away, and of the effect of the magnetic disturbances used to create and maintain these stations, have shown that they will have a definite effect on the structure of the Sun itself. We have not yet completed all our calculations, but preliminary studies indicates that if this type of solar interference is not stopped, it may cause our Sun to nova in somewhere between two and three years time."

He stopped, but the thirty-year-old prodigy, Russell Clyde, took up the story. "By nova, we mean that the Sun will literally explode. It will flame up, burst to many times its present size. Such an explosion will burn Earth to cinders, render all the planets inside the orbit of Jupiter uninhabitable, scorch their atmospheres, dissolve their waters into steam, and make them lifeless flaming deserts. We have seen other stars turn nova. We have measured their explosions. We know just about what age and stability inside a sun is necessary to cause this. And we fear that the danger of our own Sun doing so is great — if the Sun-tapping is not stopped."

Everyone at the table was silent. Burl was stunned. Finally he caught his breath. "But how can we stop it? We can't get to all the planets in time. Our rockets are not ready—and rocketships would be too slow. Why it would take two years for rocketships to reach Mars, if the expedition were ready now . . . and I understand that it will be another ten years before Operation Mars is even attempted."

General Shrove nodded. "That is correct. Our rocket engineering is not yet advanced enough to allow us to take such emergency action. We are still only just over the doorstep of interplanetary flight—and our enemies, whoever they may be, are obviously far advanced. But, as you will see, we are not entirely without hope. Colonel Lockhart, will you tell them about Project A-G?"

All eyes turned to Lockhart, who was a short, stocky man in civilian clothes. Burl realized that this man had been a colonel at one time, but remembered now that he had taken a post with one of the largest aviation companies after leaving the service. Lockhart turned cold gray eyes directly to Burl.

"We have in my company's experimental grounds one virtually untested vessel which may be able to make a flight to Mars, or any other planet, in the time allowed. This is the craft we refer to as A-G 17, the seventeenth such experiment, and the first to succeed. It is powered by an entirely new method of flight, the force of anti-gravity."

Burl hung breathlessly on his next words. "You probably know that work on the scientific negation of gravity has been going on since the early 1950's. It was known shortly after experiments had been conducted on atomic and subatomic particles that grounds had at last been found by means of which a counteraction to gravity might be set up. Early subatomic studies showed that such a force was not only theoretically possible, but that certain subparticles actually displayed such tendencies. On the basis of these first discoveries, work has been going on in the development of negative gravitational drive for at least twenty years. As early as 1956, there were not less than fourteen such projects under way in virtually all the leading aircraft industries of the United States, not to mention the rest of the world. In the last few years, at the direction of the Air Force, these projects have been consolidated, placed under one main roof, and brought to its present status, which is, we believe, the one of final triumph."

He glanced at General Shrove, who returned the glance unsmilingly. "After the successful testing of several models, a full-sized craft has been built which utilizes the new method of space drive. One such craft has been built, and only one. This ship, if it works, is at this time the only means by which hunmanity can hope to make the trips to the other places in the solar system from which the Sun-stealers are working. It is with this one vessel only that we can put their Suntap stations out of commission.

"But I emphasize again the experimental nature of this ship. What its capacities are and how well it will work is still a matter of planning-book conjecture. We can prepare the ship to take off in one week's time. I do not think, judging from what Merckmann and Clyde have said, that we can afford to wait any longer. Another such ship cannot be built in less than a year."

General Shrove spoke then. "It is already arranged that this A-G 17 spaceship is going to go. A volunteer crew has been selected; several of them are in this room." He nodded briefly to Clyde and to Lockhart: "But although these volnteers are among the best men in their fields, there isn't one of them who couldn't be replaced by someone equally skilled in the same

28

field. But there is one person on Earth right now who may just possibly be unique. This person may hold, by virtue of an experience not shared by any other human being, a special key that will render easier the task that this spaceship must fulfill."

He turned to Burl, who sat tingling with suspense. "You, Burl Denning, are apparently still carrying some sort of electronic or subelectronic charge which is attuned to the controls of the Sun-tap station. We feel that you should be along on this expedition. It will be long and dangerous, it will involve landings on worlds no man has ever visited or expected to visit for hundreds of years. There is an enemy in the sky who will certainly try to stop our single ship. To be bluntly honest, the voyagers on this ship face such dangers as explorers have not faced since the days of Magellan and Cook. Its chances of return are remote. But with the permission of your father, which he has already given, I would like to ask that you volunteer to join its crew."

Burl felt dizzy, his heart thumping painfully within his chest. He took a deep breath, and then carefully, trying to keep his voice from quivering, he said, "Yes, I'll go."

CHAPTER FOUR

The Hidden Skyport

AROUND THE table there was a concerted sigh. Burl, his ears still throbbing from his sudden excitement, realized each of them had been holding his breath. General Shrove smiled and glanced at the elder Denning, who sat expressionless. It is not an easy thing for him, Burl thought.

At that moment, Burl knew that he had come of age. This moment of decision, coming truly and literally like a bolt out of the blue, had thrust him into man's estate before his time. He would show that he was able to carry this burden.

Shrove now spoke to Lockhart. "Colonel, we are holding you to your schedule. According to it, you can take off in five more days. Will you need any more time because of this addition to your crew?"

The stocky air veteran shook his head. "Not at all. We'll be loaded and ready on the hour I set. I'll take Denning in hand and brief him on what he may need to know. Actually, we may even be able to get him a home-leave. After all, his duties won't begin until actual planetfalls are made."

They rose from their seats. Burl stood up, uncertain as to procedure, but Lockhart came over to him and took his arm. "Burl, we're going to have to give you a run-down on the ship and plans. We've no time to waste if you want to get a chance to say good-by to your folks later on."

"I understand," said Burl. He turned and waved to his father, who was in conversation with the general. "I'll see you at home in a few days, Dad," he called, then followed Lockhart out.

Outside the building they were joined by several othere members of the conference and immediately ringed about by a squad of Air Force men wearing sidearms. Burl realized that they were to be thus guarded everywhere they went. Obviously, the possibility that the builders of the Sun-traps might have agents on Earth had occured to the officers.

Russell Clyde, the young astronomer, was among their group. He walked over to Burl and shoved out a hand. "Glad to have you with us, Burl. This is going to be quite a trip!"

Clyde was about Burl's size. He had an engagingly boyish air about him, and Burl took a liking to him. Burl had heard of him before. For the young man, while still a college student, had formulated a remarkable new theory of the composition of galactic formations which had instantly focused the attention of the scientific world upon him. This theory had been taken up by the gray-beards of the scientific world and had survived the test of their debates. Now associated with the great Mount Palomar Observatory, Russell Clyde had continued to build a reputation in astronomical circles.

"You're one of the expedition then?" asked Burl, shaking his hand.

The redhead nodded. "Yep. They're taking me as their chief astrogator. And don't think it's because I'm any great shakes at it, either! It's just that I'm still young enough to take the kind of shoving around these high brass figure we're going to get. Boy, have they got it figured!"

Burl chuckled. "Ah, you're kidding, Dr. Clyde. You've probably been in on this from the beginning."

The other shook his head vigorously. "Nope. It was going to be Merckmann's baby, but when they realize they have a fight on their hands, they always look for young blood. And, say, cut out this 'Doctor' stuff. Call me Russ. We're going to share quarters, you know."

"How do you know that?" asked a tall, rather sharp-featured man who had overheard them. "The colonel will assign quarters."

"I say he will . . . and you can bet on that," snapped

Russell Clyde. He waved a hand in introduction. "This is Harvey Caton, one of our electronic wizards."

Caton nodded, but before he could continue the discussion, Lockhart rounded them all up, packed them into a couple of station wagons, guards and all, and they were off.

The next days were hectic ones. By car and plane the group was transferred to the large, closely guarded base in Wyoming where the secret anti-gravity ship was waiting. Burl did not see the ship right away. First, he was introduced to all the other members of the crew, and given a mass of papers to study which outlined the basic means of the new space drive, and which detailed the opinions and suggestions of various experts as to methods of procedure and courses of action. He was subjected to various space medical tests to determine his reactions under differing pressures and gravities. Although it proved a strenuous and exhausting routine, he emerged from the tests with flying colors.

The expedition was commanded, as he had known, by Colonel Lockhart who would also act as chief pilot. The famous military flier proved to be a forceful personality with a great skill at handling people. He knew how to get the most out of each man.

Russell Clyde was the chief astrogator and astonomical expert. Assisting him was the rather pedantic and sober Samuel Oberfield, a mathematical wizard and astrophysicist, on leave from an assistant professorship at one of the great universities. Clyde and Oberfield would also act as copilots relieving Lockhart.

Harvey Caton, blond Jurgen Detmar and the jovial Frank Shea were the three-man engineering crew. Completing the members of the expedition was another trio chosen to act as general crew, medical and commissary men while in flight, and as a trained explorer-fighter unit while on planetside. Roy Haines, of whose exploits in Africa and the jungles of South America Burl Denning had heard, was the first of these, a rugged, weatherbeaten, but astonishingly alert explorer. Captain Edgar Boulton, on leave from the United States Marines, was the second—a man who had made an impressive record in various combat actions in his country's service. The Antarctic explorer, Leon Ferrati, completed the listing. Ferrati was an expert on getting along in conditions of extreme frigidity and hostile climates. Of these men, only Lockhart, Clyde, Detmar and Ferrati had had space experience in the platforms and in Moon-rocketry.

It was still, thought Burl, a large crew for a spaceship. No rocket built to date had ever been able to carry such a load. But by then he had realized that the strict weight limitations imposed by rocket fuels no longer applied to this new method of space flight. Burl found himself more and more anxious to see this wonderful craft.

It was not until the morning of the second day that Burl's chance came. He had fallen asleep on the stiff army cot in the hastily improvised base on the Wyoming prairie where the final work was being done. The day had been a confused jumble of impressions, with little time to catch his breath. Now he had slept the sleep of exhaustion, only to be awakened at dawn by Lockhart.

"Up and dress," the colonel greeted him. "We're taking you out to look the ship over. Detmar will come along and explain the drive."

Burl threw his clothes on, gulped down breakfast in the company of the others at the messhall, and soon was speeding along a wide, new road that ran up to the mountains edging the wide western plain. As they neared the mountains, he saw a high wooden wall blocking the road and view; this was the barrier that concealed the ship nestled in the valley beyond.

They passed the guards' scrutiny and emerged into the valley. The A-G 17 loomed suddenly above them, and Burl's first impression was of a glistening metal fountain roaring up from the ground, gathering itself

34

high in the sky, as if to plunge down again in a rain of shining steel.

The ship was like a huge, gleaming raindrop. It stood two hundred feet high, the wide, rounded, blunt bulk of it high in the air, as if about to fall upward instead of downward. It tapered down to a thin, perfectly streamlined point which touched the ground. It was held uprightly by a great cradle of girders and beams. At various points the polished steel was broken by indentations or inset round dots that were thick portholes or indications of entry ports. Around its equator, girding the widest section was a ring of portholes, and there were scattered rings of similar portholes below this.

As the three men drew near the tail, the great bulk loomed overhead, and Burl felt as if its weight were bearing down on him as they walked beneath.

Two men were suspended from the scaffolding above. Burl twisted his neck and saw that the designation A-G 17 and the white-star insignia of the United States had been lettered along the sides. But what was it the men were painting now?

"It will read *Magellan*," said Lockhart, following Burl's eyes. "We've decided that that would be the appropriate name for it. For what we are going to have to do with it is not just to make a simple trip to explore another planet, but to cirscumnavigate the entire solar system."

Burl found his eyes dazzled by the vessel, hanging like a giant bulbous mushroom over them. Around him, he began to realize that a number of other activities were going on. There were spidery scaffolds leading up to open ports in the metalic sides. Workmen were raising loads of material into these ports, and for an instant Burl caught sight of Haines, in rough work clothes, shouting orders from one of the openings as to exactly where to stow something.

At last he took his eyes away from the startling sight. The little valley around him had a number of low storage shacks. A road led in from another pass through the mountains. Two loaded trucks came down this pass now in low gear. Lockhart, watching, remarked, "We are having our equipment and supplies flown up to a town twenty miles away and then trucked in."

"Why didn't you leave this ship where it was built—in your plant in Indiana—and load it from there?" Burl asked.

"It would have been easier," said the colonel, "but security thought it better to transfer the craft to its launching sight up here in these deserted hills. We are going to make our take-off from here because we are still too experimental to know what might happen if something kicked up or if the engines failed. We'd hate to splatter all over a highly populated industrial area. Besides, you must know, if you looked over those papers yesterday, that there's a lot of radioactive stuff here."

Burl nodded. Detmar cut in. "Why don't we get aboard and show him over the sthip? It will be easier to make it clear that way."

Suiting action to the word, the three went over to one of the loading platforms, climbed on the wiry little elevator, and were hoisted up fifty feet to the port in the side of the ship. They entered well below the vast, overhanging equatorial bulge which marked the wide end of the teardrop-shaped vessel.

They walked through a narrow plastic-walled passage, broken in several places by tight, round doors bearing storage vault numbers. At the end of the passage they came to a double-walled metal air lock. They stepped through and found themselves in what was evidently the living quarters of the spaceship.

The *Magellan* was an entirely revolutionary design as far as space vehicles were concerned. Its odd shape was no mere whimsy, but a practical model. If a better design were to be invented, it would only come out of the practical experience of this first great flight.

It had long been known, ever since Einstein's early equations, that there was a kinship between electricity, magnetism, and gravitation. In electricity and magnetism there were both negative and positive fields manifesting themselves in the form of attraction and repulsion. These opposing characteristics were the basis for man's mastery of electrical machinery.

But for gravitation, there had seemed at first no means of manipulating it. As it was to develop, this was due to two factors. First, the Earth itself possessed a gravitational phenomenon in this force outside of that intense, all-pervading field. Second, to overcome this primal force required the application of energy on such scales as could not be found outside of the mastery of nuclear energy.

There was a simple parallel, Burl had been told the day before by Sam Oberfield, in the history of aviation. A practical, propeller-driven flying machine could not be constructed until a motor had been invented that was compact, light and powerful enough to operate it. So all efforts to make such machines prior to the development of the internal combustion engine in the first days of the twentieth century were doomed to failure. Likewise, in this new instance, a machine to utilize gravitation could not be built until a source of power was developed having the capacity to run it. Such power was found only in the successful harnessing of the hydrogen disintegration explosion — the H-bomb force. The first success at channeling this nuclear power in a nonbomb device had been accomplished in England in 1958. The Zeta-ring generator had been perfected in the next decade.

Only this source of harnessed atomic power could supply the force necessary to drive an A-G ship.

The nose of the *Magellan* housed an H-power stellar generator. Within the bulk of the top third of the ship was this massive power source, its atomic components, its uranium-hydrogen fuel, and the beam that channeled the gravitational drive.

"Negating gravity is not a simple matter like inventing a magic sheet of metal that cuts off the pull of the Earth, such as H. G. Wells wrote about," Oberfield had explained. "That is impossible because it ignores all the other laws of nature; it forgets the power of inertia, it denies the facts of mass and density. It takes just as much energy to lift an anti-gravity ship as to lift a rocketship. The difference is only in the practicality of the power source. A rocketship must burn its fuel by chemical explosion in order to push its cargo load upward. Its fuel is limited by its own weight and by the awkwardness of its handling. This A-G ship also must supply energy, foot-pound for foot-pound, for every foot it raises the vehicle. But due to the amount of energy supplied by this new generator, such power is at last available in one compact form in such concentration that this ship could propel itself for hundreds of years."

He went on to explain that what then happened was that the vessel, exerting a tremendous counter-gravitational force, literally pushed itself up against Earth's drive. At the same time, this force could be used to intensify the gravitational pull of some other celestial body. The vessel would begin to fall toward that other body, and be repelled from the first body—Earth in this case.

As every star, planet, and satellite in the universe was exerting a pull on every other one, the anti-gravity spaceship literally reached out, grasped hold of the desired gravitational "rope" hanging down from the sky, and pulled itself up it. It would seem to fall upward into the sky. It could increase or decrease the effect of its fall. It could fall free toward some other world, or it could force an acceleration in its fall by adding repulsion from the world it was leaving.

In flight, therefore, the wide nose was the front. It would fall through space, pulled by the power beam generated from this front. The rear of the spaceship was the tapering, small end.

As Burl was shown over the living quarters it became plain to him that the actual living spaces in the *Magellan* were inside a metal sphere hanging on gymbals below the equatorial bulge that housed the power drive. The bulk of this sphere was always well within the outer walls of the teardrop, and thus protected from radiation. Being suspended on gymbals, the sphere would rotate so that the floor of the living quarters was always downward to wherever the greatest pull of gravity might happen to be.

Burl and the others explored the three floors that divided the inner sphere, all oriented toward Earth. The central floor, housing the sleeping quarters and living quarters, was compact but roomier than might have been expected. There were five bunkrooms, each shared by two men. There was a main living and dining room. On the lowermost floor was the cookroom, a small dispensary, and immediate supplies. On the upper floor was the control room, with its charts and television viewplates which allowed vision in all directions from sending plates fixed on the surface in various areas.

In the spaces between the inner sphere and the outer shell were the basic storage areas. Here supplies and equipment were being stocked against all possible emergencies. In the tapering space of the tail below the sphere was a rocket-launching tube. Stored in the outer shells were various vehicles for planetary exploration.

Haines came into the control room where the three were standing. He was wiping his hands on a piece of cloth, and looked tired. "Finally got the special, sealed-engine jeep stowed away," he said. "I was afraid we weren't going to get it in time. The Moon-base people had ordered it, and they're going to holler bloody murder when they find out we appropriated it."

Lockhart shrugged. "Let 'em yell. It'll be too late when they find out. How much longer will we need before you finish the loading?"

Haines drew a chair up to the chart table and sat down. "I expect to get some more stuff tomorrow, and then the two-man rocket plane the next day. We already have the four-man rocket aboard. That'll do it. The rest of your men ready?"

Lockhart nodded. "We're just about set. Denning

here can take a quick trip home tomorrow, and we'll be ready the day after."

Burl looked about him quickly. One day, two days, maybe a third—and then, the plunge into the unknown. Detmar reached upward and drew down a metal ladder hanging in the curved ceiling of the chamber. "I'm going to take a look in the engine room," he said. "Want to come along?" he asked Burl.

Before the young man could say yes, Lockhart shook his head. "No, I don't want him to. I don't want anyone going up there who doesn't have to. That stuff is shielded, but you can never be sure."

Burl was disappointed, for he had wanted to see the nuclear generators. But Detmar shook his head, smiled, and pushed aside a round trap door in the ceiling. Burl could see that it connected with a similar door a foot higher. Detmar pushed it open and ascended into the forbidden sphere of the Zeta-rings. Burl got a glimpse of subdued, bluish light, and then the trap door shut after the engineer.

Later as they drove out through the valley, Burl looked back at the huge ship, and now, instead of appearing like an overhanging metal waterfall, he saw it as a widenosed bullet, aiming at the sky, surging against its bonds—a bullet for humanity's sake.

CHAPTER FIVE

Up the Rope of Space

BURL'S VISIT home was a curious interlude. Actually, he had been away only a few weeks, since the summer vacation had begun, yet this single day had an air about it different from that of any other homecoming. He found himself continually looking at things in a more inquisitive, more thoughtful manner.

That which had been commonplace was suddenly something valuable, a sight to be treasured. For he had realized, as he sat in the fast plane transporting him home, that the Earth was itself a planet among planets, and that this might possibly prove to be his last visit to town where he had been born. He had pondered, as he had gazed out of the ship's windows, just what it could mean to depart from this world and travel among the uncharted reaches of empty and hostile space . . . to set foot upon planets where no human foot had ever touched and to meet unguessable perils.

So his home, his mother, his friends, the street on which he lived, took on a novel air. He studied them while enjoying a quiet day at home. He watched the cars in the street, so amusingly compact and small, each designed in the fleeting style of the year. The cars of a dozen years ago had been designed for length and size, but the trend had been the opposite for a decade now. The cars grew smaller and their lines weirder as the manufacturers strove to compete.

What other planet could boast of such simultaneously astonishing ingenuity and wondrous tomfoolery?

He looked at the people going about their business, the other boys of his age intent on their summer jobs and summer fun, and wondered if he would ever be able to join them again without the cares of a world on his shoulders?

People were unaware of the crisis that hung over the solar system. There had been news of the dimming of the Sun, but the meaning behind it had been carefully screened, and the expedition was a top secret. It availed the world nothing to panic about this matter. Now the odd weather quirks had been forgotten, and the main subjects on people's tongues were the baseball scores and the latest telemovies.

When Burl kissed his mother and father good-by, it was with a sense that he was also kissing good-by to his youth, and entering upon a new period of the most desperate responsibility.

This mood lingered with him back at the base, although his companions of the trip to come seemingly did not share it. On the last day, quarters had been assigned in the *Magellan*, and the men moved their belongings to their tight bunks in the heart of the ship. Clyde had his way, and he and Burl shared a double-decker chamber.

There was a hustle and bustle in the valley. The supplies seemed unending, and Burl wondered why the variety. "For once, we've got lifting power to spare," was Russ's comment. "Nobody knows what we're going to need on the various planets, so Lockhart is simply piling aboard everything he can think of. You'd be amazed at the space we have for storage. And Caton says that the more we stick in there, the better the shielding is against the radiation belt surrounding Earth —and probably the other planets as well."

"I thought we were already well protected," said Burl. "With the atomic generators, we had to be shielded anyway. Haven't we lead lining all around our inner sphere quarters?"

Russell Clyde nodded. "Oh, sure, but the more the merrier."

He and Burl were already in their quarters, stowing their clothes. "We leave in an hour," said Burl. "Are we going to the launching base at Boothia, where the manned rockets go up?"

Clyde shook his head. "Lockhart talked it over with

42

us yesterday, and we decided to take off from right here." By "us," Burl knew the operational group was meant, which consisted of the colonel, the two astronomers, Caton as head of the engineering section, and Haines. "To tell the truth, nobody knows how easily this ship will handle. We're shielded well enough so that a short passage through the radiation belt three hundred miles up and for the next fifteen hundred miles shouldn't have any effect on us at all. The rockets, which can't be shielded because of the weight limitations, have to go up at Boothia because there, at the North Magnetic Pole, there's a hole in the radiation."

Boothia Peninsula was a barren spot far up in the Arctic Zone on Canada's frozen eastern coast. On it was constructed the world's major space port—a lonely outpost from which rockets departed for the equally lonely Moon bases. Burl had read about it and had looked forward to seeing it, but realized that the flight of the *Magellan* marked still another change in the fast-altering history of the conquest of space.

The hour passed quickly. The little valley was cleared of visitors. The crew was called to take-off posts—Lockhart at the controls, Clyde and Oberfield at the charts, Detmar watching the energy output. The rest of the crew had been strapped into their bunks. By special request, Burl was observing in the control room, seated in a half-reclining position like the others, in a well-padded chair, strapped tight.

Haines had remarked as he had supervised the strapping-in, "Nobody knows whether this is going to be necessary. But we're taking no chances." He'd gone to his quarters and done the same thing.

Lockhart watched the registering of the dials in front of him, waiting for the load to build up. There was a muffled whine from overhead as the generators built up current. Detmar called out a cryptic number every few seconds and the colonel checked it. The two astronomers were idle, watching their viewers. They'd made their calculations long before.

"Time," called out the colonel, pressing a button. A

gong rang throughout the quarters. He moved a lever slowly.

Burl waited for the surge of pressure he had read always occurred at take-off. But there was no such pressure. He lay back in his seat, gripping the arms. Gradually he became aware of a curious sensation. He seemed to be getting lightheaded, and to tingle with unexpected energy. He felt an impulse to giggle, and he kicked up his foot to find it surprisingly agile. About him the others were stirring in their seats as if caught by the same impulses.

Now he felt loose against his bonds and he became a little dizzy. There was a pounding in his head as blood surged within him. His heart began to beat heavily.

"We're losing weight," muttered Clyde from his chair, and Burl knew the ship was tensing to take off.

The great generators were beginning to push against Earth's gravity and, as their force moved upward to match Earth's, the weight of everything in their sway decreased accordingly. Lockhart's first move was simply that—to reduce the pull of Earth to zero.

In a few moments that point was accomplished. A state of weightlessness was obtained within the *Magellan*. Those watching outside from bunkers in the surrounding mountains saw the huge teardrop shiver and begin to rise slowly above its cradle of girders. It floated gently upward, moving slowly off as the force of Earth's centrifugal drive began to manifest itself against the metal bubble's great mass.

Everyone on the crew had experienced zero gravity, either in the same tests Burl had undergone or on actual satellite flights, and thus far, no one was too uncomfortable. The entire structure of the ship quivered, and Burl realized that the inner sphere which housed their air space was hanging free on its gymbals.

Lockhart rang a second gong, then turned a new control. The pitch of the generators, faintly audible to them, changed, took on a new keening. The ship seemed suddenly to jump as if something had grasped it. The feeling of weightlessness vanished momentarily,

44

then there was a moment of dizziness and a sudden sensation of being upside down.

For a shocking instant, Burl felt himself hanging head downward from a floor which had surprisingly turned into a ceiling. He opened his mouth to shout, for he thought he was about to plunge onto the hard metal of the ceiling which now hung below him so precipitously.

Then there was a whirling sensation, a sideways twisting that swung him about against the straps. As it came, the room seemed to shift. The curved base of the control room, which had been so suddenly a floor, became in a moment a wall, lopsided and eerie. Then it shifted again. and, startlingly, Burl sagged back into his cushioned seat as the hemispherical room again resumed its normal aspect.

Lockhart bent over the controls, cautiously moving a lever bit by bit. Clyde was bent over his viewer, calling out slight corrections.

Now, at last, Burl felt the pressure he had expected. His weight grew steadily greater, back to normal, then increased. He found himself concentrating on his breathing, forcing his lungs up against the increasing weight of his ribs.

"Hold up," his buzzing eardrums heard someone say —possibly Oberfield. "We don't need to accelerate more than one g. Take is easy."

The weight lessened instantly. Then the pressure was off. Everything seemed normal. Lockhart sat back and began to unloosen his straps. The others followed suit.

In one viewer, Burl glimpsed the black of outer space and in another, the wide grayish-green bowl of the Earth spreading out below. In a third he saw the blazing disc of the Sun.

"Did everything go all right?" he asked quietly of Clyde.

The redhead looked up at him and smiled. "Better than we might have expected for a first flight," he said.

"We're latching on to the Sun's grip now. We're falling toward the Sun; not just falling, but pulling ourselves

45

faster toward it, so that we can keep up a normal gravity pressure. We're soon going to be going faster than any rocket has ever gone. The living-space sphere rotated itself as soon as we started that. That's what made everything seem upside down that time and why everything has come back to normal."

Burl nodded. "But that means that in relation to Earth we are ourselves upside down right now!"

"Of course," said Clyde. "But in space, everything is strictly relative. We are no longer on Earth. We are a separate body in space, falling through space toward the Sun."

"Why the Sun?" asked Burl. "I thought our first objective was to be the planet Venus?"

"It was too hard to get a fix on Venus from so near the Earth. Instead, we latched on to the Sun to pull us inward. When we are near to Venus' orbit, we'll reverse and pull in on Venus," was the astronomer's answer.

"Is'nt that rather risky?" asked Burl, remembering some of the quick briefings he had been given. "That's a departure from your plans."

Lockhart looked up quickly. "Yes, you're right," he admitted. "But on a trip like this we've got to learn to improvise and do it fast. We made that decision at take-off."

For an instant Burl felt a chill. He realized then what all the other men on the ship had known all along—that in this flight they were all amateurs, that everything they did was to be improvisation in one way or another, that they must always run the risk of a terrible mistake.

Had latching on to the Sun been the first such error?

CHAPTER SIX

Sunward Ho!

GRADUALLY THE ship settled down to routine. There was, as Burl discovered, nothing very much to do for most of the crew on such a space flight. The course was charted in advance, a pattern laid out that would carry the ship falling toward its objective—falling in a narrow curving orbit. A certain amount of time would pass during which the ship would traverse a specific section of this plotted route at a certain rate of speed or acceleration.

Then, at a specified moment, the speed would be checked, the attraction of the Sun reversed, and the ship would attempt to brake itself and to halt its fall toward the great Sun. At such a time as its fall came to a stop, it should, if the calculations had been correct, be crossing the orbit of the planet Venus in the same place and at about the same moment that Venus itself would be. In that way, the ship would arrive at the planet.

Now all these calculations had been made, and once made, set into motion on the control panels of the ship. The interval of many days between actually left little to do, except for making astronomical observations, checking on the performance of the stellarators, setting a watch against the damage caused by meteors and micrometeors, and following the ordinary procedures of meals and sleep periods. The men set up an Earth-time schedule of twenty-four hours, divided the crew into three eight-hour shifts, and conducted themselves accordingly.

Burl did not find time weighing on his hands. Despite the limited space available to the ten men, there was always something to learn, and something to think about.

When Russell Clyde was off duty, he spent much time with Burl at the wide-screen viewers that showed the black depths of interplanetary space surrounding them. The Earth dwindled to a brilliant green disc, while ahead of them the narrow crescent of approaching Venus could be seen growing gradually. Ruddy Mars was sharp but tiny, a point of russet beyond the green of Earth. And the stars—never had Burl seen so many stars—a firmament ablaze with brilliant little points of light—the millions of suns of the galaxy and the galaxies beyond ours.

On the other side, the side toward which they fell, the Sun was a blinding sphere of white light, its huge coronal flames wavering fearfully around its orb.

Seen to one side, surprisingly close to the Sun, was a tiny half-moon. "That's Mercury," said Russ, pointing it out. "The smallest planet and the closest to the Sun. After we leave Venus, we'll have to visit it. We know there's a Sun-tap station there—and because it's so close to the Sun—its orbit ranges between twenty-eight million miles and under forty-four million miles —the station must be a most important and large one."

Burl gazed at the point of light that was the innermost planet. "Those Sun-tap stations . . . The more I think about it, the more I wonder what we're up against. It seems to me that it ought to be easy for the kind of people who can build such things to catch us and stop us. In fact, I wonder why they haven't already gone after us for stopping the one on Earth?"

Russ whistled softly between his teeth. "We've some ideas about that. The military boys worked on it. You know you can figure out a lot of things from just a few bits of evidence. We have such evidence from what happened to you on Earth. You ought to speak to Haines about it."

Burl turned away from the viewer. "Let's find him now. I don't think he's very busy. He said something about catching up on his reading this period."

Russ nodded, and the two of them got up from their

seat. With a wave to Oberfield and Caton on duty at the controls, the two climbed down the ladder that led into the middle part of the living space. They looked into Haines's quarters but he wasn't there. So they went down the next hatchway into the lower section.

Haines and Ferrati were sitting at a table in the cooking quarters, drinking coffee. The two men, both heavy and muscular, used to the open spaces and the feel of the winds, were taking the enforced confinement in the cramped and artifically oxygenated space of the ship will ill ease. For them, it was like a stretch in jail.

They greeted the two younger men jovially and invited them to a seat. While Russ poured a cup of coffee for himself, Burl opened the subject of how much the expedition had worked out about the enemy.

Haines's pale blue eyes gleamed. "You can know an awful lot about an enemy if you know what he didn't do as well as what he did do. If you figure out what you yourself should have done under the same circumstances, and know he didn't do, why, that gives you some valuable hints as to his deficiencies. As we see it, we've got a fighting chance of spoiling his game. Certainly of spoiling it long enough to allow Earth several more years to get a fleet of ships like this into operation and give him plenty of trouble."

Suddenly Burl felt more cheerful. At the back of his mind there had been a carefully concealed point of cold terror—he remembered the clean efficiency of the Suntap station, the evidence of a science far beyond that of Earth. He pressed the point. "Just what do we really know?"

Haines leaned back and rubbed his hands together. "There were several things that gave their weaknesses away. When we put it all together, we decided that the enemy represents some sort of limited advanced force or scouting group of a civilization still too far away to count in the immediate future. We decided that the enemy isn't too aware of our present abilities—that his intelligence service is poor as far as modern Earth is concerned. We figure he won't be able to act with any speed to repair the damages we make."

"Tell them how we worked that out," said Ferrati, who had begun to grow again the short black beard that Burl remembered he had worn on his famous expeditions.

"Well," said Haines, drawing the word out to build up suspense, "did you know that the station in the Andes, the one you cracked open, was built at least thirty years ago? And never put into operation in all that time?"

Burl was surprised. "Why . . . I hadn't thought of it —but it could have been. That valley was so isolated and deserted, probably nobody would ever have spotted it.

"Right," Haines added, "and our investigation team studied the remains, the foundations, the layout, and we're sure it's been there at least three decades. That's one clue.

"The second clue was the relative flimsiness of the walls. The builders hadn't expected us to be able to blow them up. They were some sort of quick construction—a plastic, strong, but not able to hold up against blasting powder, let alone real heavy bombs or A-bombs.

"Now why was that? And the third clue, why didn't they have a repair system available, or at least some sort of automatic antiaircraft defense?"

Burl looked at Ferrati. The latter was watching him shrewdly to see if he could figure it out.

"The builders didn't expect an air attack," said Burl slowly, "because of the air disturbances. They did not know we would have a Moon base that could spot their location. Hence they figured that our civilization would remain as it was thirty years ago. We wouldn't have been able to spot the location at that time, because it required outer-space observation. It might have taken us several years of tramping around to locate it."

"And the lack of a strong permanent construction? After all, a concrete and steel-enforced embankment, which any military force on Earth could have put there, would have balked your dynamite attack," prob-ed Haines.

"That means they didn't have the time or the means to make such a construction. They must have had a single ship with the kind of equipment that could lay out a quick base in the shortest time!" said Burl.

"Right!" snapped Haines. "The Sun-tap must have been built by a relatively small team, which probably came in a single explorer ship. The ship was equipped with automatic factory machinery that could turn out an adequate base for an uninhabited planet, an airless moon, and so on—but they didn't have the stuff for a fortified base—and they didn't have the manpower to build it."

"Another indication of that is the thirty-year delay," added Ferrati. "Obviously, they arrived in this solar system from somewhere outside it. We figure that way because otherwise they would have been prepared to do the job on all the planets in the same trip and start operations at once. They must have made some obser-vations of this solar system from a point in space at least as far away as another star. That means not less than four and half light-years away—Proxima Centauri being the nearest star after our Sun, and four and a half light-years from us. Their observations were imperfect. They found more planets and problems than they had supposed. So they had to make a second trip to get enough supplies to finish their Sun-tap base construc-tions. It took them thirty years between the first sta-tions and the ones that completed the job.

"And that, too, suggests that only one ship was origi-nally involved here. Of course, maybe they came back with more the second time, but it still looks as if the main force hasn't arrived. And won't until after the Sun novas."

"Then that means," said Burl quickly, "that we are still dealing with just a small and isolated group?"

"Maybe," said Haines. "Just what constitutes a small group may be hard to say. I rather think they'd have brought the engineers and at least an advance working party of settlers with them the second trip in. But they are still short of available ships—they're still not aware of what we may be going to do."

"Why is that?" asked Burl.

Haines looked thoughtful. "This is conjecture. But if they planted any spies among our Earth people, there's been no contact, because otherwise they'd have known we could track and crack their base as soon as it started. This means that they still haven't had scouting ships to spare for checking up on what they did the first time. No checkup means no spare personnel to do the checking. They just assumed that we hadn't caught on, and started operations by remote control as they had originally planned."

"And that also may mean that these people are hard up," said Ferrati. "Wherever they came from, their civilization has been great, but it's gone to seed. They plan to seize another solar system, start over again, and they haven't the abundance of material needed to set up simple check and guard stations, such as any major Earth nation would have the sense to do."

"Why, that means we've got a fighting chance to lick 'em," said Burl joyfully. "I kept thinking we'd run into more than we could cope with."

"We've got a fighting chance, all right," said Haines. "We may be able to rip up their Sun-tap layouts, but what if we meet the main explorer ship itself? Anybody who can cross interstellar space and warp the power of the Sun, can probably outshoot, outrun, and outfight us. Let's hope we don't meet them until we've done our work."

On this note the little discussion broke up as the gong rang for the next watch.

It made sense to Burl. If the *Magellan* could just operate fast enough, keep on the jump, they'd save the day. But—and he realized that nobody had mentioned it aloud—it also followed that the enemy—however small its group—was still in the solar system somewhere and would certainly be starting to take action very soon now.

The time came when the ship was to start slowing, to prepare itself for the meeting with Venus. Burl saw the hour and minute approach and watched Lockhart take the controls and set the new readings. The steady hum of the generators—a virbration that had become a constant feature of the ship—altered, and for everyone it was a relief. Their minds had become attuned to the steady pitch. One didn't realize how annoying a nuisance it was until it stopped. As the stellar generators let down on the drag on the Sun, the gravity within the ship lessened. In a few moments there was a condition of zero, and those who had forgotten to strap themselves down found that they were floating about in the air, most of them giddy.

There was a shift in the pitch, and the generators applied repulsion against the pull of the Sun. Those floating in the air crashed suddenly against the ceiling, then slid violently down the walls onto the floor as the inner sphere rotated on its gymbals to meet the new center of gravitational pull—this time away from the Sun.

The viewers flickered off and then on again as their connecting surfaces inside and outside the sphere's double layer of walls slid apart and matched up again. For an instant, as he saw the viewers blank out, Burl thought of what might happen if the sphere didn't rotate all the way. They would find themselves blind.

Now the ship proceeded on its charted orbit, slowing to meet Venus. Several hours went by, one meal, and Burl had returned to his bunk, his rest period having arrived. Russ remained at the controls on duty, checking astronomically the new speed and deceleration.

Burl tossed restlessly, the light out in the little cabin. Something was bothering him, and after a while he realized that Clyde should have come off duty before this. He glanced at the clock and calculated that Russ was two hours overdue. What was wrong?

He slipped out of his bunk and climbed into his

pants. Ascending into the control room, he saw Lockhart, the two astronomers, and the entire engineering crew gathered over the controls in worried concentration.

He peered over their shoulders, but the dials meant little to him, since he did not know what they should have said. "What's happened?" he asked Russ.

Russ took his aside. "We're not going to make our connection with Venus," he said. "Our generators didn't operate exactly as we had hoped. We haven't been able to slow down enough, the pull of the Sun is stronger than the power we can raise to stop it at our present speed. We're going to shoot past Venus' orbit way ahead of the planet, and we're still heading sunward at a faster rate than we figured on."

"You mean—we're falling into the Sun!" gasped Burl.

"As things stand right now," said the youthful astrogator, "that's just what is happening."

CHAPTER SEVEN

Hot Spot on Mercury

IT SEEMED strange to Burl at that moment that there wasn't more excitement on board the *Magellan*. To learn so early in the game that all were doomed should have brought more reaction. It should have excited some sort of frenzy, or efforts to abandon ship, or something. But the men in the cabin, though keyed up, were anything but panicky.

Instead, there seemed to be grim concentration on their faces, an earnestness that spoke of a plan. Through a viewer which had been shielded so that the light would not blind the eyes, Burl could see the wide disc of the Sun now. A few spots were visible on its blazing surface, and great tongues of burning gases encircled it for hundreds of thousands of miles. Were they really destined to end a mere cinder—an instantaneous flicker of fire in one of those prominences?

Clyde was working with Oberfield at the calculators. Burl watched them in silence, trying to determine what it was they were getting at. Finally they pulled a figure from one of their machines and took it over to Lockhart and the engineers. There was a brief conference, and something seemed to be agreed upon.

Clyde's face, which had been tense, was now more relaxed. "I think we've got the problem licked," came the good word.

"What's up?" asked Burl. "If we shoot past Venus, we should still be able to come to a stop, fall away from the Sun and maybe catch up with Venus again. It would take longer, but . . ."

"We're altering our plans," interrupted Russ. "Of course, we could brake—that much we found out for sure. The trouble lay in our lack of effective tests for the *Magellan's* drive. We thought we knew just what it would do, but after all, the problems of space are intricate. It turned out that it did not act so effectively against the Sun as had been calculated. Either that, or the Sun's pull was stronger at this proximity than registered on our instruments. Chasing after Venus, after coming back to its orbit, could be done, but it would prove time-consuming and difficult to plan. What we are doing instead is altering our schedule."

"But then there's no other place to go from here but Mercury. Is that what the new plan is?" Burl asked him.

Russ nodded. "Mercury is coming around this side of the Sun. By the time we have braked, we will be closer to its orbit than to that of Venus. So we shall proceed inward toward it and make our first planetfall there."

Mercury, the smallest and hottest planet in the system. Burl remembered that it was one of the two worlds that they knew for sure had a Sun-tap station on it. He went down the hatch to carry the news to the landing crew.

Haines, Burl discovered, had already heard the new plan on the intercom from Lockhart. As soon as Burl joined them, the four men, including Ferrati and Boulton, went into a planning session.

The problem of Mercury was a hard one. As Ferrati remarked, "It would have been better to tackle this one last instead of taking it on first."

"Yes, but on the other hand," was Haines's comment, "Mercury's station is probably one of the most important—located as it is, so close to the Sun. With ideal conditions for steady, undiverted concentration of solar power, it must be the primary station in the system."

"The problem boils down—and I do mean 'boils'—to heat," Boulton laughed. "Mercury rotates on its axis only once a year—its year being only eight-eight of our days long. This means that just as the Moon presents only one side to the Earth, Mercury always presents the same hemisphere to the Sun. On the Sun side, therefore, there is always day. The Sun appears to be fixed in the sky. Naturally, we assume the Sun-tap station will be on that sunny side. And the heat must be terrific."

"Matter of fact," said Haines dryly, "the records show the heat in the center of the Sun side reaches 770° Fahrenheit. Enough to keep tin and lead molten."

"The problem is how to reach the station over such a boiling landscape," summed up Burl. "It seems to me that the absence of an atmosphere could answer part of the problem."

Haines nodded. "Let's get to work on a plan of action, men. We've got a few days to get our equipment laid out."

Those few days passed quickly enough. When several possible schemes had been outlined, the men made lists of the types of equipment that might be used with each. Then, putting on pressurized space suits and carrying air tanks, they left the inner sphere and worked through the cargo space surrounding it within the outer frame of the spaceship. There had originally been air here, but now they found most of it was gone, thinned out from infinitely tiny leaks in the outer shell caused by the constant bombardment of microscopic bits of meteoric dust.

They located each piece of equipment and moved it into position for easy handling.

The ship came to its halting point, where the repulsion against the Sun finally braked it against the gravitational pull of the Sun. Then, by increasing the selective pull of the approaching planet Mercury, they moved off in that direction.

Mercury was changing in appearance. As they neared it from the outer side, its lighted half swung away from their view, and what they saw was a constantly narrowing crescent, growing larger even as it narrowed. Finally the hour came when they swung up close, coming in on the eternally sunless, night side of the little planet.

They swooped low over the dark surface, taking observations and measurements. "It's not as cold as we might suppose," said Oberfield after his first readings.

"There's a certain amount of heat all along the rim of the dark side. Radiation, I suppose, as well as the fact that there's a certain amount of wobbling done by the planet."

Burl was studying the surface. "Seems to me that much of the dark side has a gleam to it. Something reflects the stars; I see little glints of light, shifting and blinking."

"I can guess what that is," said Russ. "It must be covered, at least in the central portions, with a sea of frozen gases. What atmosphere Mercury had long ago must have congealed there."

The ship moved along toward the twilight edge, then began circling the planet along that intermediate belt, where the Sun could be seen peeking over the horizon in eternal dawn. There was a cluster of men at the radiation counter, looking for evidence of the Sun-tap station. Finally, after passing over a chain of darkened mountains, eerily lighted at the peaks by the Sun, there came a yell. Distortion had been detected.

Once on it, they swung the ship outward into space again and moved along further over the sunlit side. Burl stared into the telescopic viewers as they probed the surface.

He saw an ugly and terrifying world. The planet, which had a diameter of only 3,100 miles, compared to Earth's 7,900, was virtually without an atmosphere. Its surface was baked hard, brilliantly white, covered with long, deep cracks that cut hundreds of miles into the shriveled and burned surface. There were areas of dark mountain ranges, bare and jagged, whose metallic surface imparted a darker shade to the pervading glare. And there were patches here and there on the surface that gleamed balefully—probably spots of molten material.

Haines, standing next to him, was muttering, "It can't be too far in, it can't. How could they build it?"

Then Burl found what they were looking for.

A huge canyon tore raggedly across a plain. There was a jumble of mountains, a chain edging in from the twilight zone. And in a corner, about two hundred miles out into the hot side, at a narrow ledge where the mountains came down and the canyon came together, there was a circular structure.

They could see, as soon as the telescopic sight had been adjusted, that it was a large station. It was encircled by a featureless wall. It had no roof. Rising on masts above it was a whole forest of gleaming discs pointing at the Sun low in the sky.

On the tops of the mountain peaks, a half mile from the station, was another series of masts. These were aimed away from the Sun into the dark airless sky and toward the other planets.

"The accumulators and the transmitters," said Burl. "We'll have to get them both."

"Getting the transmitters will be easy," said Haines. "After we shut off the station, we'll just bomb the mountain masts out of action."

Burl choked. "Why, it never occurred to me, but why can't we bomb the station from the air? One atomic bomb should finish it off." He almost added, And you wouldn't have needed me after all, but squashed the thought. He wouldn't have given up coming along for anything, he now realized.

"There's a distortion, as there was at the Andes station, that would make it hard to hit. But I imagine we could do it if we tried hard enough. But that isn't what we want at first. It's important, very important, that we get pictures and details of this station from inside. We can't just break up the enemy installations—we've got to learn from them, we must find out how they do it and how we can use it." This was Lockhart speaking. "You'd better start the job," he added to Haines. "Are you ready?"

Haines nodded reluctantly. "Yep," and turning to the three who would accompany him, he ordered, "let's go."

The four explorers gathered near the exit port. They had put on space suits and strapped on various items of equipment, weapons and work tools. They passed through the airlock into the cargo section of the ship. Communicating through the helmet radios, Haines directed each what to do, and also directed Lockhart where to bring the ship for the landing.

Burl heard Lockhart's voice warn them that he did not want to hold the ship too long over the sunny hot side. "We've already noticed a buildup of heat from the solar radiation on the skin. And the heat radiating from Mercury is accumulating too fast. We can't get rid of it if *both* sides of this ship are going to be heated up. As soon as you make your landing, I'm taking the ship back to the cold side."

"Uh huh," came Haines's voice. "We don't want to hang around here any too long, either."

Then the four, as prearranged, unlimbered the work rocket they had picked. There were several sizes of small exploration craft. They had at first thought of the tractor—an enclosed, airtight truck on tractor wheels which could crawl up to the station while the men inside it were protected by air conditioning. But a quick survey showed that it would overheat too fast and might easily bog down in one of the many soft spots. So they took the four-man, rocket-propelled cargo plane instead.

The ship was airtight and pressurized. They had taken every precaution. The four piled in with their supplies. Then, as the *Magellan* swooped momentarily lower, the escape hatch opened and, with Ferrati at the controls, the rocket plane shot out with a roar of its exhausts.

They raced low over the burning landscape, and before them the wide, dark, forbidding canyon cut its way through the plain. It was into this canyon that the rocket plunged.

The precipitous rocky sides rose above them, and suddenly they were in darkness. Immediately, the plane's cooling system became more effective as Ferrati guided the rocket through the shadowy depths away from the blazing sunbeams. Burl saw, by means of the radar, that the bottom of the heat crack was many miles down.

They raced along the crevice until they reached the mountain chain. Here, Ferrati abruptly raised the nose of the plane and they shot upward, popping out of the shadow into the sunlight.

Before them loomed the hard unbroken walls of the Sun-tap station. The rocket plane came to a stop a hundred feet away.

As soon as it had halted, Burl and Ferrati leaped out, with white sheets thrown over their suits to afford some extra protection from the Sun's rays. Between them they carried a long, awkward affair of poles and plastic.

Burl's feet touched the ground; through the cushioned leather of his thick boots he felt the heat just as if he had stepped on a hot stove. He moved quickly, and as they had rehearsed, he and the explorer slapped the rig together and set up a gleaming plastic skin sunbreak to shield the rocket plane. The plastic sheets reflected the Sun's heat and cut off a fair portion of the direct radiation which would otherwise have rendered the rocket plane inoperable and uninhabitable in short order.

While they were assembling the sunbreak, Haines and Boulton unloaded a portable antitank rocket launcher. With no wasted motion, Boulton aimed the launcher at the wall, and Haines thrust a long, wicked-looking rocket projectile into the tube. There was a flash of soundless fire and a line of dissipating white smoke. Nothing could be heard in the airlessness.

Burl felt the shock through the ground as the shell hit. A chunk of the wall ripped apart and collapsed.

As quickly as he saw it, Burl acted. Haines's voice rang in his ear, but already Burl was in action. Back into the rocket plane, out again with—an umbrella!

He made a flying leap toward the Sun-tap station. He felt terrifically strong in the slight gravity, and the leap carried him thirty feet forward. As he slid through the space above the surface, he opened the umbrella. Its outer side had been painted white, and partly shielded him from the direct heat. He made the station in five leaps and climbed through the broken wall.

Boulton followed him with another umbrella and a pack under his arm.

Inside the station it was cool—the walls had been high enough to create shade within. It was like the station in the Andes, but bigger, much bigger.

Boulton joined him, folded his umbrella calmly, and yanked an air-compression pistol from his belt. "See anyone?" he asked.

"No."

Burl remembered then that there could possibly be a living guard at this station. They searched carefully, but there was no sign of life. Boulton was doing a soldier's job, that was all.

While Boulton set up his photographic equipment, Burl made his way around the shining globes and strange tubes that were the nerve center of the station. He finally found the same type of control panel that he had found in the Andes station.

He hesitated before it, wondering if, after all this, the original charge, would work. He hoped that there might be another charger globe available, but saw none. It would be up to him.

He put a gloved hand on the control. Perhaps, he worried, the charge would not conduct through the insulated, cooled material of his suit. He pushed the levers, and knew then that it did.

The pulsing of the spheres halted. There was a sharp dip in the faint vibration he had been feeling in his feet. He shoved the levers all the way, and suddenly the station went dead. Above him, one of the great discs atop its mast snapped the burst apart under what must have become an impossible concentration of power without a channel for outlet.

"Sun-tap Station Mercury is dead," Burl said quietly into his helmet phone.

At that very instant a distant globe, perched on a pedestal against the wall away from the rest of the equipment, flared a brilliant red.

CHAPTER EIGHT

The Veil of Venus

IN AN artificially constructed chamber somewhere in the solar system, an intelligent being sat before a bank of instruments that was designed to bring to his attention various factors concerning the things that mattered to his species. This being had been on duty for the average length of time such a duty entailed and had been paying little conscious attention to the routine— for there had been nothing to report for some time.

The drop in channeling from Planet III that had occurred some time ago had thus far not caused too much concern. It was assumed by the other intelligent beings involved that the matter was possibly a weather condition, a volcanic discharge or quite simply that the planet was in unfavorable orbit. Not all the stations ever worked simultaneously. There were always some behind the Sun, or blocked in some other manner. But the main channels were at work, and the different lines and shifts continued to build up satisfactorily.

But now something occurred that focused the attention of the watcher more closely on his instruments. A facet of his panel had flashed a color at the lowest end of his visible spectrum. How the being registered that color cannot be said; the inhabitants of Planet III would have termed it red.

With trained reaction, the watcher activated the full signal. Instantly there appeared before his eyes a vision of a scene. There was the interior of the major station on Planet I. It was non-functioning, and there were two strange creatures turning now to look directly at him. They were bipeds with two armlike extensions, lumpy objects, clad in bulky white folds. They wore cumbersome helmets and he could see two eyes shielded beneath thick transparencies over the face.

One of these creatures raised his arm and there was a puff of steam. Then the vision flashed off, but not before the trained watcher had activated the crash mechanism.

If the watcher had been closer in space to the station, the destruction would have come quicker. Unfortunately for him, the speed of light and radio impulses is limited, so that it was several minutes before the destruction impulse reached Planet I.

A short while later, after the guiding beings had digested the news, preparations were made for a vessel to go sunward to investigate—and remove—the interference.

Burl twisted on his heel sharply as he whirled around to look at the flash of red. Boulton drew his hand weapon, aimed and fired.

There was a jet of steam as the compressed air blasted the dart from the gun. The glowing globe was pierced, there was a small explosion, and then the globe and its pedestal vanished.

"What was that?" cried Burl.

Boulton hostered his gun. "A signal of some kind—a warning probably. My guess is that it was an alarm tipping off the remote control masters of this place that it was out of commission. Help me with the photo stuff; I think we'd better get out of here quick!"

Without wasting more time, the two men snapped the scene as fast as the shutters would click. Then they picked up the cameras, grabbed their umbrellas and ran for the break in the wall.

Just as they made their first flying leaps toward the shielded rocket plane, the globes within the Sun-tap station started to go off. One after another, like a chain reaction, they blew up, and within seconds the interior of the walled station was a turmoil of falling metals, beams, wires, and sharp transparent shards.

Haines and Ferrati were ready for take-off and puffs of smoke were coming from the exhaust. Without bothering to take down the plastic Sun-shield, Burl and

Boulton tumbled into the cabin. Before the door was even closed, Haines lifted the ship and headed for the dark depths of the canyon.

The inside of the plane was perilously hot. The shield had been a temporary protection, but even the ground radiated heat like an oven. They had to seek the cold of the sunless canyon to allow some of the heat to escape. To have flown directly to the *Magellan* without cooling the plane would have been disastrous.

The *Magellan* emerged from the cold side to meet them. From the heights of space, they saw that they would not need to bomb the mountain relayer masts— for the same alarm that had triggered the station had shattered them.

After the *Magellan* had scuttled back to the cold side, there was a council of war in the control room. Burl and Boulton described very carefully what had happened.

"This must have been their primary station," said Russ thoughtfully. "No matter what they seek to channel from the Sun on other planets, it is from here that the first and strongest diversion of solar energy must have been coming. This station may have been the last constructed—the final link put into place. And for that reason, they installed an alarm."

"Ah," said Lockhart, "even if they did, would it necessarily have destroyed that station? After all, they would normally have figured on repairing whatever went wrong."

"It seems to me," said Burl, "that the red flash it-self didn't start the destruction. There was a delay— must have been several minutes—before it started. Could it be, that what was alerted was a watcher?"

"Where?" said Boulton. "There was no place for a watcher to be in that station. We saw no sign of it."

"Maybe deep underground?" suggested the engineer, Caton. "They might have living quarters a few miles underneath."

"Highly unlikely," said Russ Clyde. "It would still be too hot, and, remember, these people plan to incinerate

Mercury and the inner planets. They must be from the edge of the system. The delay may be a valuable clue to that. It would take time for a remote control station or another planet to see what was happening and take steps. If you can figure out exactly how many minutes and seconds elapsed between the flashing of the red bulb and the blowup, we could work out the approximate distance."

But, unfortunately, the time could not be judged that accurately. Neither Burl nor Boulton had had time to look at his watch.

They hung over the cold side of Mercury for several hours more while the two astronomers figured their next move. When the orbits had been determined, the *Magellan* turned its massive wide nose away from the Sun toward a gleaming white disc that dominated the dark skies of outer space. With full power on, they pushed away from the littlest planet and began the long fall toward the Sun's second planet, that which some had considered to be Earth's veiled twin, Venus.

There was a matter of thirty million miles to cross, and the crossing would be made fighting the pull of the Sun all the way.

Caton and his men had spent the wait on Mercury working on the great generators in the powerhouse nose. They recalibrated the output and corrected it from the records kept during the flight inward. Now they were confident of its ability to drive the ship away from the Sun. Coming in, they had not been sure what their A-G drive would do and could do. Going outward they knew just what to expect.

They did not travel blindly outward, for that would have been both a crude waste of power and inaccurate. Instead, the ship drove at a long slant from the Sun, moving in a gently curving orbit that would bring it onto Venus at the same time that Venus itself was moving along in its orbit. This is what they had tried to do before, but without success. Venus travels around the Sun at a speed of about 32 miles per second, and takes about 224.5 days to complete the circuit. From where the *Magellan* took off, it would approach and overtake Venus at a speed a little greater than the 32 miles per second.

The days passed swiftly enough. They had developed the pictures taken in the Mercury station, and the engineers and astronomers spent long hours debating their features, matching up what they had seen with what was known about the Andes station.

The shining face of Venus grew larger. It was a mysterious planet, the most mysterious in the system, even though it was the closest of the planets to Earth. Venus was a world whose atmosphere—of Earthly depth —was a solid mass of clouds. Never had the clouds lifted to reveal the surface. The clouds reflected the sunlight brilliantly, yet as Burl could now see with the naked eye, parts of it were hazy, as if mighty storms were raising dark particles from below.

"We've had a couple of prober rockets shot into its surface," said Russ, as they watched the oncoming planet. "They didn't prove much—faded out fast, but we think they established its length of day. Nobody knew how many hours it took Venus to rotate on its axis. Some even thought it always presented one face to the Sun as does Mercury. Others thought it had a quick day, shorter than Earth's. Others gave it a day almost a month long.

"Our prober rockets, carrying unmanned instruments, rather definitely indicate that the planet has a day about twenty Earth-days long. Even though it's shielded by the clouds, it must be miserably hot near the surface."

"We'll soon find out." Burl grinned. "After Mercury, it couldn't be so bad. Maybe it rains all the time."

Russ shrugged. "Who knows?" he said.

Venus was a vast sea of swirling white and gray clouds beneath them when the *Magellan* reached it. They hung above the cloud level, while stretching below them lay the circular bowl of veiled mystery that was the fabled evening star of poem and song.

Oberfield was probing the surface with the radiation counters for the Sun-tap distortion. None had been detected from Earth, but observation of the sunny face of Venus had always been difficult from the third planetary orbit. But quickly the dour astronomer proved the fact. A calculation of the planet's albedo—its rate of reflected sunlight—showed that in one large central section there was a dimming out. Somewhere in that spot, the light was being diverted.

Lockhart brought the *Magellan* down gradually, closer, closer, and finally sank it into the soupy atmosphere of Venus. Now, from every viewplate, nothing reflected but a glare of white mist. But the ship was not operating blind. Radar pierced the clouds, and from the wide screens the crew could see that they had not yet touched the surface.

"Watch out for mountains," whispered Russ, hanging over Lockhart's shoulder.

Their progress was slow but steady. The cloud bank around them did not clear, but still glowed gray. After a descent of nearly two hours, there was a flicker on the radar. It registered no features, no mountains, nothing but a seemingly flat plain.

Above and around them the white clouds still blanketed everything. But now Burl thought he saw a pale glow. Gradually the white faded away into wisps and shreds, and in a flash the ship broke out of the clouds.

They hung beneath a grayish-white sky. Below them, scarcely a half mile of visibility in misty, thin air, they saw the surface of Venus. They were over water. An ocean stretched below them as far as the eye could see, with neither a rock nor an island. Venus was a water world!

CHAPTER NINE

The Ocean Primeval

THE MAGELLAN hung in the air while the men studied the surface of this world that had so long been a mystery. The air was not the clear air of Earth; rather, it was the kind that precedes the coming of a fog, thick, heavy with moisture, the horizons fading into gray. Below them lay a mottled expanse of water, reflecting the gray sky, and verging almost to a deep brown. The water was still, occasionally stirred by a slight wave.

"No tides have ever moved these waters," commented Russ quietly to Burl. "There is no moon to pull and sway them. The motion of this world, so slow in the passage of its day, hardly disturbs the water."

"It looks shallow to me," said Burl. "The darker sections look as if the bottom must be close."

"I imagine it is. We'll take soundings," Russ answered. "I have a feeling the whole world may be like this . . . one vast, shallow, swampy sea. See the scum floating on it?"

"See it? Now that you mention it, there's hardly a part that hasn't something on it." was Burl's reply. "There're patches of muck all over it, like floating oil, or even drifting masses of weeds."

It was true. The water showed on its surface a strange filth unlike anything one would expect on the surface of a Terrestrial sea. There were wide areas of brownish-gray slime and little floating blobs of green. Shining flecks of yellow, like bright oil drops, seemed to flow through and between the masses of scum.

At the radar, Haines began to call out figures. As Russ had guessed, it was a shallow sea. In places, the bottom was only a dozen feet beneath. For a while, all the men of the crew were quiet, watching the silent waters beneath them.

"Unclean, the whole place looks unclean," Lockhart said finally. "We've got work to do. Let's find the Sun-tap station."

The rest of the crew came to action. The spaceship began to move slowly, while Oberfield and Caton probed for the lines of force which would lead to the station.

Now a long, low bank appeared, a ridge of mud protruding above the water. Here and there stretched other low mud bars, and once a ridge of rock.

"I've seen no animals or birds," said Burl. "Do you suppose there are any?"

Russ pursed his lips. "I don't think so. From the look of this world, life probably isn't developed that far. You won't find animals until there is dry land—and I'd guess now that there's no place on all Venus where there is much dry land. There may be fish or fish life, but even that's questionable. Consider—the long, long day, the absence of violent, unshielded Sun rays, the steady damp warmth, the quiet, barely moving waters, the heavy amounts of carbon dioxide in the air . . ."

He paused and went over to Lockhart's chart table to pick up a paper. "Oberfield worked out the atmosphere. It is very heavy in carbon dioxide, very low in free oxygen. There's water vapor down here, but the clouds have kept it below; it didn't show up in the outer atmosphere at all."

"There's the Sun-tap base," said Burl, and added as an afterthought, "I think."

This one did not look at all like the other stations he had seen. There was indeed a ringed wall station, but the wall was low and slanted outward. It stood on the end of a wide mudbank, and near it veins of rock glistened as if wet.

The interior machinery was a neat, compact mass of crystalline globes and levers. But the masts and shining discs which had characterized the stations on Mercury and Earth were missing. Instead, there floated upon the surface of the water, for a mile around, great shining bowls, like huge saucers gently rocking in the faint wavelets. Thin, flexible, shining lines of metal connected this surface layout with the station.

"With no direct Sun to aim at, this station seems to be directed toward a nonfocused system of light diversion," Lockhart announced. "The wrecking crew please get under way!"

"I'm going down with you," Russ joined in. "I've gotten permission to take some observations from the surface."

"Good," said Burl, and hurried with him down to the central floor.

They disembarked in two parties. Haines and Ferrati used the two-man rocket plane and would make a wide encirclement of the vicinity, mapping and finally blowing up the accumulator discs floating on the surface. Burl, Russ, and Boulton took a helicopter.

The helicopter, under the control of the Marine captain, dropped out of the cargo port of the *Magellan*. Steadied by the regular whirl of its great blades and driven by tiny rocket jets in the tip of each wing, the whirlybird swung down like a huge mosquito hovering over a swamp patch.

It moved over the water and finally hung directly over the mudbank. Maneuvering so that the helicopter was directly in the protected circle of the walls, Burl and Russ dropped a rope ladder and swung down hand over hand to be the first human beings to set foot on Venus.

They were lightly dressed, for the temperature was hot, around 110°, and it was humid. No breezes blew here. They wore shorts and shirts and high-laced leather boots. Each carried two small tanks of oxygen on his back. A leather mouth nozzle strapped across the shoulders guaranteed a steady flow of breathable air. In their belts were strapped knives and army pistols. Russ carried recording equipment, and Burl a hatchet.

They dropped off the swaying ladder inside the station. The ground was hard-packed as if the builders had beaten it down and smoothed it off. The globes were familiar to Burl—he had studied the pictures of the two he had already visited and he realized that they follow-

71

ed the same general system. Where the mast towers would have been, there were leads running through the plastic walls out across the sea. He wondered briefly why the walls were curved outward.

As the helicopter moved away, the metal weight on the end of the dangling ladder brushed the top of the wall. There was a crackling noise, and a spark jumped between them.

"The wall is electrically charged," said Burl. "I wonder why?"

Russ shook his head. "From the looks of it, to keep off something. Perhaps some kind of native life. But what? I'm sure there's nothing of a highly organized physical structure here."

Burl found the controls of the station, but before touching them, he remembered the alarm on Mercury. "I'd better try to smash the alarm first," he called out to Russ.

Finally, Burl located an isolated globe perched on a post, which resembled the one he had briefly glimpsed on Mercury. He ran his hands over it, feeling a mild vibration within. Then, at its base, he found the levers. He moved them and the vibration died out. "I think I've turned it off," he announced. "But stand by with a gun, just in case."

Russ drew his pistol, and Burl switched off the main controls of the Sun-tap. A globe or two burst; there was a sort of settling down in the station. Abruptly they felt the heat intensify and knew that the sky was shining more brilliantly than before. The diversion of the Sun was over for Venus.

The alarm globe remained quiet, but Burl took his hatchet and smashed it. Russ was carefully photographing the station, measuring the distances, and tracing the lines. Overhead, the wide blades of the helicopter flapped around and around, accompanied by little hissing puffs of rocket smoke. They could see Boulton looking down at them from the tiny cabin.

Russ was scooping up bits of soil to bring back for analysis when he saw what seemed to be a wet patch on top of the wall. As he watched, it spread until it reached the bottom. In a remarkably short time a whole section of wall was gleaming wet. A patch of damp oiliness spread over the floor.

"This I've got to get a sample of," said the rusty-haired astronomer. He reached for a sampling bottle in his pocket, and at the same time the patch of wetness spread to his shoes.

As Russ stepped forward, there was a sucking sound, and he lifted a thick gummy mass that was stuck to his sole. He shook his foot, set it down, and lifted the other, but it, too, was imbedded in thick slime. The stuff now was running up his ankle.

"Hey!" he called out, and swung one foot vigorously to free it. More swiftly that he could move, the whole patch slid down the wall and swept around him. It was moving up his legs, as if trying to envelope him.

"It's alive!" he shouted, and grabbed for the knife in his belt. In vain he tried to slash out. "It's like a giant amoeba that engulfs its food! Get it off me!"

But the knife was ineffective. He fired his pistol, but the thing was just a vast wide puddle of slime, without brain, heart or organ that could be harmed. The soles of Russ's boots were already half eaten away and his socks were going fast. Some of it was touching the skin of his knees.

He screamed as the stuff burned him.

Burl had joined the attack with his knife, but leaped back when that proved useless. His mind raced for a way to help. Above them, Boulton was swinging the helicopter down so Russ could hoist himself out of harms' way, but time would not permit it. In another instant the mass would have Russ.

Burl grabbed at the straps crossing his shoulder and swung the two oxygen tanks from his back. He snatched one from its leather holster, and pointed its nozzle at the mass of slime. He turned the stream of oxygen on, and then, taking his pistol, held its muzzle in the jet of oxygen and fired it.

The roar of the gun was matched by the roar of a

stream of fire that shot from the tank. Wherever the burning jet of oxygen touched, the mass shriveled and blackened. Yards and yards of amoeba seemed to writhe, hump upward in agony, and pull away.

There was a ring of burned white along the ground, a sickening smell in the air, but the thing was dead.

Russell Clyde grabbed the ladded as it swung toward him, and climbed up. The soles of his boots were gone and the sides were strings of raw, half-eaten leather. His legs and knees bore ugly patches of red where the slime had touched.

"Well done!" called Boulton to Burl from the cabin. "Come on up before something else comes along!"

Burl grabbed the ladder. He took two steps on the swaying, swinging rope as the helicopter started to climb and suddenly he felt himself losing strength. He become dizzy and tried to hold on, but began to lose consciousness. Dimly he heard Boulton yell at him, "The oxygen, the other tank, turn it on!"

The second tank was still dangling from his chest.

Fighting for consciousness, Burl twisted the nozzle. There was a hiss and he felt air blow against him. Miraculously, his senses cleared, and holding the oxygen tank tight against him, he climbed up the ladder and into the safety of the helicopter.

CHAPTER TEN

The Dying Planet

RUSSELL CLYDE was confined to his bunk during the next four days, his feet wrapped in bandages and ointment. Fortunately the digestive juices of the Venusian amoeba had only just begun their attack upon the skin after eating through the footgear. Except for some painful blisters and rawness, his condition was not serious.

The little stateroom was cramped, containing as it did two bunks, one above the other, like the cabin of a liner. What with a couple of built-in lockers for clothes, and a bolted-down chair and a reading lamp, it was not a place to spend any more time than necessary. The lack of a window added to the inhospitality of the room. But Burl had accepted long ago the fact that a spaceship could not yet be considered a luxury liner. In time, the A-G drive would permit such things, but the *Magellan* was an experimental vessel turned by emergency into a warship.

During those four days, Burl spent most of his time with Russ, getting to know him better, and talking about the trip. The young astronomer was not at all chagrined by his misadventure. In fact, the whole experience had him quite buoyed up.

"What a wonderful place for biologists to study! Venus will be a Mecca for scientific learning!"

"But not for anything else, I don't think," said Burl. "Anyway, we're in for another experience now. Mars is our next goal. What's it like?"

Russ put his hands behind his head and looked up at the bottom of the bunk above him. "We can see Mars well enough; there's no cloud blanket and the atmosphere is thin but clear. You've seen the photos and the colored sketches?"

"I've seen it from our viewplates, but so far it's just a tiny, red disc. We're about at Earth's orbit now, even though Earth is many millions of miles away from us. Mars is still about fifty million miles further, but we're gaining speed quite rapidly and Lockhart thinks we'll make it soon enough." Burl picked up one of the books from the ship's library and started to thumb through it to locate a color chart of the planet.

Russ waved a hand. "You don't have to show me. I've studied Mars by telescope so often I know it by heart. It's mostly a sort of light, reddish-tan, a kind of pale russet. We think that's desert. There are some fairly large sections that are bluish-green—at least in the Martian summers. In their winters these sections fade very greatly."

"That's vegetation," Burl broke in. "It must be! Everybody agrees it acts like it. And there are the white polar caps, too."

"You can tell which season is which by the size of the polar ice caps. When one is big, the other is almost gone. Then there's the problem of the canals . . ."

"Do you believe in them?" asked Burl. "The books disagree. Some think they're real—even say they look as if they had been built by intelligent beings as irrigation channels to take the melting waters of the poles down to the fertile lands. But other astronomers claim they can't see them—or that they're illusions, series of cracks, or lines of dark dust blown by winds."

"Personally, I've come to believe in them," Russ argued. "They've been photographed—something is there. They're very faint, spidery lines, but they certainly are straight and regular. We'll find out soon enough."

Find out they did. Russ was up and about and the normal life of the ship resumed. During their passage of Earth's orbit, they had manager to raise the United States on the ship's radio. For three days they were able to converse with their home base. They exchanged news and data, transmitted back all they had learned and eagerly asked for news.

The men of the crew had the chance to send messages home, and Burl even talked briefly with his father. There had been an important discovery made on Earth.

The lines of force had finally been traced. The distortions visible on Mars, as well as the one from Mercury before its cutoff, had been worked out directionally. There was no doubt that a line of force had been channeled outward to a point in space that now proved to be that of a planet. The planet was Pluto.

"Pluto!" That was the shocked word uttered by everyone within hearing distance when the radio voice said it.

"Pluto! Why, that's the end of the line! The most distant planet," said Oberfield, shocked. "We'll have to go there—all the way!"

That fact sobered everyone. It meant the trip must last many times longer than anyone had expected. But they were a band of men who had achieved great things —they had managed so far to work together in harmony, and they felt that since they had conquered two planets—what were a few more?

Mars gradually grew larger on their telescopic viewers as the *Magellan* fell onward through space, riding the beam of gravity that was like a pulling rope to them. The slow down and reverse was made in good order—the sphere swinging around, readjusting, and the great, driving Zeta-ring generators now pushing and braking.

Then one wake period, Russ and Burl went to the telescope and trained it again on the oncoming planet. The now large disc of the ruddy world swung onto the screen. It looked strange, not at all like the drawings.

Burl had never seen it through Terrestrial telescopes, but he sensed something was wrong. He realized suddenly, "Both poles are enlarged! It's winter on *both* hemispheres! And that's impossible!"

Yet it was so. Both the Martian ice caps were present and both extended down the northern and southern hemispheres of the world. The men stared in silence.

Slowly Russ tried to figure it out, "The greenish-blue areas can scarcely be seen. Where they should be, there're darker patches of brown, against the yellowish-red that now seems to be the desert areas. It seems to be winter on both sides and it looks bad. It looks to me as if Mars were a fast-dying world."

Burl squinted his eyes. "Yet I see the canals. The straight lines are still visible—see?"

Russ nodded. "They're real. But what's happened?"

Indeed, the planet seemed blighted. "It's the Sun-tap," Burl decided. "We should have realized what it would do."

"Remember Earth the week it was working? The temperature fell several degress, began to damage crops? Remember how it snowed in places where snow had never fallen in July? Remember the predictions of disaster for crops, of danger from winter snows if the drop continued?"

Russ went on in his careful, explanatory way. "And for Mars it has continued. Mars was always colder than Earth; life there must have been far more precariously balanced. During the day, on the Martian equator in midsummer, the highest temperature is not likely to be more than 70° or 80°; and at night, even then, it would fall below freezing. Vegetation on Mars must have been hardy in the best of times, and life carried on under great difficulties.

"Now the margin of warmth and light has been cut. It has been just enough to keep both polar caps frozen, to prevent water from reaching the fertile regions, and the cold has advanced enough to bar the growth and regeneration of plant life. If the Sun-tapping on Mars is not stopped, all life there will die out, and it will be a permanently dead world forever."

The news spread throughout the crew and there was a feeling of anger and urgency. Nobody knew what lived on Mars, yet the subject of Mars and Martians had always intrigued the imaginations of people on Earth. Now, to hear that the unknown enemy had nearly slain a neighboring world brought home vividly just what would also have been the fate of Earth.

The day finally came when the big spaceship slid

into an orbit about the ruddy planet. It circled just outside the atmospheric level while the men aboard studied
the surface for its secrets.

Mars was indeed inhabited. This fact was borne
home by the canals and the very evident artificial nature of their construction. They could see clearly
through their telescopes that there was an intricate
global network of pipelines, pumping stations, and irrigation viaducts from pole to pole. They also saw that
at the intersections of the canals were dark sections
crisscrossed with thin blobs of gray and black which
proved under the telescopes to be clusters of buildings.
There were cities on Mars, linked by the waterways.

They saw no aircraft. They detected no railroad lines
or roadways beyond the canalways themselves. The
many regions of darker, better ground, intersected by
the canals which no longer fulfilled their purposes, were
covered with thick vegetation—forests of dying, wintery
stalks. Only a flicker of dark green here and there
showed where some faint irrigation still got through.

They saw also that there were lines of white, which
had not been visible before. Snow was gathering in low
spots, and the planet was freezing up.

The lines of solar distortion were strong, and they
traced them to their point of concentration. The point
was not some isolated spot far in a desert, away from
Martian investigation. To the amazement of the men,
the location of the Sun-tap station was actually within
a Martian city!

"Do you suppose," Lockhart queried the others, "that
the Martians themselves are the builders of this setup—
that this is their project—that they are the criminals
and not the victims?"

There was no answer. The evidence was apparent, but
it made no sense. If the Martians had created this
thing, it was destroying them. And yet, if they had not
created it, why did they—so clearly a race that had at-
tained a high level of engineering ability—tolerate its
continual existence?

As the ship descended, they saw the city emerge. It

consisted of hundreds of gray mounds—buildings laid out in the form of neat hemispherical structures, like skyscraper igloos, with rows of circular windows. Each building was like the next, and they fitted together in a series of great circles, radiating outward from the meeting spot of the canals.

The explorer crew waited at the ship's rocket launchers for an attack. The tail of the teardrop housed the built-in armament—the rocket tubes which could send forth destruction to an enemy. But though Haines sat with his finger on the launcher button, no aircraft rose to meet them from the city below. No guns barked at them. No panic started in the streets.

They could see tiny dots of living beings moving about, but no sign of alarm, no evidence that they had been noticed.

Even here, at the equator, there were streaks of white snow in the streets and rings of rime along the bases of the buildings.

Directly below them lay the Sun-tap station. The lines converged here, and the rings of distortion could be seen in the atmosphere, causing the city to flicker as if from the presence of invisible waves.

Then they saw the masts and their shining accumulators projecting about a cleared spot near the outskirts of the city. The customary walled ring and the open machinery were not visible.

"The Sun-tap station is under the city!" said Lockhart, shocked. "It's been built beneath the streets somewhere, and the Martians walk around above it and let the masts alone! They must be the builders!"

"If so, why are they killing themselves?" Burl couldn't see the sense of it. "And if they have reasons, then why don't they defend it? They were alerted while we were on Mercury. They must have spaceships if they are the enemy. Where are they?"

The ground was now but a few hundred feet below them, and still no one paid the strange ship hanging in the sky any attention. While the crew stood with bated breath, Lockhart brought the ship down and down,

until it came to rest barely fifty feet above an intersection. There it hung, nearly touching the roofs, and
was ignored.

The shining masts of the Sun-tap station continued
to gleam, following the tiny bright Sun in its course
through the dark blue of the sky. One of the two small
Martian moons was climbing upward along the horizon.
The canals beyond were dark lines of conduit, through
which no life-giving waters flowed. And the Martians
did nothing.

CHAPTER ELEVEN

Martians Don't Care

I DON'T like the looks of this at all," said Lockhart finally. "I suspect a trap. Yet we've got to land and get at that base. I'm going to take the ship out into the desert beyond the city and let a scouting squad go in first."

The *Magellan* lifted back into the sky, then moved out over the ocher wasteland that was the barren desert of the red planet. Slowly the ship dropped again until its pointed nether end hung about twenty feet above the cold shale and time-worn sand.

Captain Boulton and Ferrati were selected to do the initial survey. Burl and Haines helped them climb through the packed spaces of the outer hold. The jeep was swung out to the lowermost cargo port, and the spaceship's cargo derrick lowered the compact army vehicle to the ground.

The two scouts then put on altitude suits with oxygen masks, slung walkie-talkies about their chests, took light carbines in hand and pistols in belts and went down the rope ladder from the cargo port. They climbed into the sturdy jeep with its specially-designed carburetor and pressurized engine. The vehicle had been prepared to operate in the light atmosphere of Mars, as thin as the air on a Himalayan mountaintop, and low in free oxygen.

Burl and Haines, clad in pressure suits themselves, sat in the open port and watched the jeep set off. The engine kicked over and barked a few times in the strange air. Then Boulton at the wheel threw in the clutch, stepped on the gas, and the squat little car, painted in Air Force blue, rolled off over the flat rocky surface, kicking up a light cloud of sand as it went.

On Haines's lap sat a walkie-talkie. Boulton and Ferrati kept up a running commentary as they approached the city. Ferrati described the ground and the appearance of the oncoming city.

The jeep was now a small object merging with the dark mounds of the city's outermost buildings. "We haven't met any Martians yet," came Ferrati's voice. "Apparently they aren't interested in investigating us even now. And here we are rolling right up to the city limits." There was a pause.

The walkie-talkie emitted a series of squeaks and squawks, and Ferrati's voice came through now with distortion. "We're crossing the city limits—there's a sort of hard, plastic pavement that begins at the very edge. Now we're going down an intersection between the buildings."

The squawks became increasingly louder. They could hear only a word or two. Haines asked whether he was getting through to them, but he could not make out an answer because of the racket.

"It's the Sun-tap station. It's generating distortion. We'll have to wait until they return," said Burl.

Haines nodded and turned off the set which had begun to utter ear-piercing howls. The two men waited quietly for about half an hour. Only a phone call from the curious men in the control room interrupted their vigil.

Then finally Burl spotted a little cloud of dust on the horizon. "There they are!"

The two men stood up as the little jeep made its way back over the desert to the ship. As it drew closer, they saw a third occupant sitting in the back with Ferrati. Haines opened the walkie-talkie. "Wait till you see this fellow," Ferrati's comment came through.

The jeep drew up to the ship and stopped. Ferrati waved them down. A few seconds later they were joined by Lockhart and Clyde, also in pressure suits.

The creature in the back of the jeep was a Martian. They stared in fascination. It was about three feet long with a small, oval-shaped head and two very large, many-faceted eyes. A small, beaklike mouth and short, stubby antennae completed its face. The head was attached by a short neck to a body that consisted of three oval masses joined together by narrow belts, much like the joints of an insect. A pair of arms, ending in long three-fingered hands, grew from the first segment. A set of long, thin legs grew out of each of the two other segments. A glistening grayish-blue shell, its skin, covered it from head to foot.

At the moment, this particular Martian was tightly restrained by a strong nylon net, and was obviously the captive of the two explorers.

"Why, it looks like a giant insect!" exclaimed Burl.

"More like a kind of lobster," was Ferrati's answer. "But this is it. This is one of the city dwellers."

Lockhart shook his head. "I don't like this. We shouldn't do anything to antagonize the Martians. Taking one prisoner like this may be a bad first move."

Boulton stepped out of the jeep. "There wasn't anything else we could do. Besides, who said that Martians were ever our friends?"

"We got into the city," he went on, "and drove around the streets. There were plenty of these fellows around, going about their business. Hundreds of 'em. Do you think they stopped to look at us? Do you think they were curious? Do you think they talked to us? Called the police? Did anything at all?

"No," he answered himself. "They just walked around us as if we were a stick of something in the way. They don't say anything to each other. They just go on about their affairs, dragging things, carrying food, herding young ones, and not a darn word.

"They looked at us, and didn't even act as if they saw us. When we stopped one, it squirmed out of our grasp and walked away. Finally we took this fellow, simply grabbed him off the street, tied him up, stuffed him in the jeep and kidnaped him. And do you think anybody cared or turned in an alarm or tried to help him? No!"

Lockhart looked at the prisoner a moment. The

Martian stared at him out of his unwinking multiple eyes. "Are you sure these are the engineers of the canals, the builders?"

Boulton nodded. "Definitely. We saw some of them at work. They were repairing a house and they used tools and fire. They have machines, and they use them. They've got their city working and well laid out, but I don't know how they do it. They must communicate in some way, but they act as if they had been drilled in their jobs and were going through an elaborate and complicated pantomime. Even the young don't utter a peep."

Lockhart stepped back a bit. "Untie this fellow. Let's see what he does."

When the Martin had been released from the enveloping net, it made no effert to communicate. It turned slowly around, a little wobbly at first, and wandered off, paying no attention to the men, the ship, or the jeep. Then it started walking at a rapid pace. The men watched as it trotted into the desert—away from the city! It seemed to wander around as if lost, and then set out in another direction, but still one that would not take it to the city which was quite plainly in view.

The Martian disappeared from view behind a series of small hummocks, still bound for nowhere.

The men were lost in amazement. Russell Clyde uttered a low whistle. "Burl's right. It must be a sort of insect."

"This whole civilization seems to be insectlike, if you ask me," said Burl. "It's like a huge anthill, or a big beehive. It seems complicated, and the creatures go through complex activities, and all the time it's something they were born with."

Ferrati nodded. "Now that you mention it, that's exactly what the city was like. Nobody gave orders—everybody just did what they were supposed to do. Nobody was curious about us because it wasn't their business."

"And, individually, they haven't intelligence," Clyde added. "That one—the one you took away from his work—plainly is lost. He doesn't know how to go about getting back. He has no curiosity about us . . . he may not even have much of a brain. Individual ants have no brain—only a sort of central nerve center. Collectively, they perform wonders; individually, they are quite helpless."

Lockhart interrupted the discussion. "Well, then, let's get on with it. Obviously, the Sun-tap builders placed their station in this city because it was a safe spot, protected by the Martians themselves, and because the Martians would never think to interfere with them. So you men can go back, take your stuff, dig out the station and put it out of commission. Get going."

Haines and Burl climbed into the jeep with Boulton and Ferrati. Russell Clyde insisted on joining them, and Lockhart gave his consent. Off they went, rumbling over the sand toward the city of instinct.

Burl was excited and curious about the Martians. They presented a strange mixture of contradictions. "How," he asked Russ, "could they have built a world-wide network of canals, set up pumping stations, laid out plantations, mastered hydraulic and power engineering, if they are mere creatures of instinct? Surely there must be brainy ones somewhere? A thinker species?"

"Not necessarily," said Russ. "Remember, these creatures are operating without opposition—they are really the highest type of life here. The need to conserve water and continue their hive life forced them to learn a practical kind of engineering. Nobody knows how the ants and bees formed their complex societies—there are none among them with any larger brains than the rest, and they do not talk. But somehow ants and bees communicate and somehow they act as a mass. Figure it on a world-wide scale, driven by the threat of their world drying up, and these creatures built up a mechanical civilization to meet it. But it also accounts for why they have never flown, not through the air and not through space, why they haven't attempted radio communication with Earth, and why they don't understand what the Sun-tap station is doing to them. Their world is being killed, and they literally haven't the brains to understand it."

They reached the city. All about was a silent hustle and bustle of enigmatic, shining, shelled creatures. Superficially, it looked like an intelligent civilization. There were wheeled carts driven by some sort of steam generator. Steam-driven engines ran factories.

The Martians made way for the jeep with unconcern. Never had they seen creatures as large as themselves that were not of their own kind on hive business. Hence, none such could exist. This was a world totally without individualism, a civilization without a spoken language, without names, without banners. Wherever or however the mass knowledge was located or transmitted, no individual of another species could ever hope to know. It would be forever as remote from human explorers as the farthest star on the farthest galaxy.

They drove to where the Sun-tap masts rose from the ground. The men parked the jeep out of the way of the silent traffic, climbed out and walked into the rounded door of a building. Its architecture was not like that of the other buildings. Inside the chambers were dark.

"These creatures have no lights," remarked Boulton. "They must use their feelers indoors."

"Ah, but look," said Burl, reaching out a hand to a little globe set on a pole in the floor. He touched it and the globe lighted up. "The Sun-tap builders needed light and put in their own fixtures here. I recognize their style."

The five men followed a hallway that sloped down into the ground, and came out into a large underground cellar—several hundred feet wide. It was the Sun-tap station. There were the now-familiar globes and rods, the force fields, the controls, the pedestals and the ends of the rotating masts.

They made their recordings, and Burl got ready to turn off the station. Ferrati and Haines uncrated a small, tactical atomic bomb they had carried with them —one of the smallest perfected by the Army during the past half dozen years. They laid it down in the center of the equipment and set the timer for a half hour away.

Boulton found the alarm globe and prepared to blow it up. Then Burl took the control panel and switched off the station. They heard the thud of a crumbling mast. Boulton fired a shot into the alarm globe which had begun to turn red. It smashed.

"All right, men," snapped Haines, "let's go!"

As they moved toward the exit, Boulton hesitated. "Hey," he said, "there's one globe still in action!"

The others turned in time to see Boulton stride over to a very small globe which was glowing pale yellow against the wall near the doorway.

The Marine captain drew his pistol, aimed and fired. The globe burst, but as it did so, a level bolt of yellow light shot back along the path of the bullet. For a split second, Boulton was outlined in yellow fire. There was a flash like lightning.

Each man reached for his weapons, but the underground station remained dark and dead. Their flashlights turned on Boulton. The stocky Marine was lying on the ground.

They ran to him. "He's alive!" cried Haines, as he saw that Boulton was still breathing, his breath whistling back and forth through the oxygen mask. Quickly Haines examined him. "His heart's all right. He's just been knocked unconscious."

Ferrati and Haines picked up the captain by his arms and legs. Though he would have been heavy on Earth, his weight on Mars was very slight, and each man knew he was capable of carrying great loads with his Earth-attuned muscles. Then, in single file, they left the cellar and came out of the doorway of the building.

As they emerged they were stopped short. Surrounding them was a tremendous and growing crowd of Martians. A solid wall of shell-like faces stared at them, and a small forest of short antennae waved and flickered in great agitation.

As they pushed their way with great difficulty toward the jeep, the crowd began to sway, as if in anger.

Now, for the first time, they heard the creatures make a noise—a sort of humming and buzzing like angered bees.

"They see us now," muttered Haines. "I don't like it."

"The Sun-tap builders did it," said Burl. "They must have booby-trapped the place against intruders. The globe that got Boulton must have set off some sort of vibration that enrages these creatures. And it looks as if we're the victims."

As they reached their jeep, the encircling mass of Martians moved forward. The humming rose to a higher pitch, and then the mob, with the berserk ferocity of a swarm of bees, lunged toward them.

CHAPTER TWELVE

At Rope's End

WITH BOULTON lying across the back seat, the four men acted simultaneously. Thinking only of self-defense, they drew their pistols and fired point-blank into the monsters attacking them. As the men emptied their guns, the Martians in front stumbled, fell, rolled over, or began to run aimlessly as the heavy slugs tore through them.

They were not easy to kill—which was to be expected of creatures without much of a central consciousness— but on the other hand, once struck or injured, they seemed to lose contact with their fellows and to act wholly without direction. They plunged wildly into each other, and before the men in the jeep had finished their barrage, the clearing was a milling, confused mob. Body clashed against body, legs scrambled under legs, and the angry buzz was now lost amid the clattering and banging of shell against shell.

Haines slid into the front seat behind the steering wheel, stepped on the gas, and drove toward a momentary gap in the mob. The jeep tore through, raced around the corner, and headed down an empty street. Crouching in the back, Burl, Russ, and Ferrati hastily reloaded.

"We can't let ourselves get stopped, or even hole up. That A-bomb's going to go off in about twenty minutes, and we'd better be back at the ship before then," cried Russ.

As they bumped along, they noticed that the Martians who came within fifty feet of their jeep suddenly stopped whatever they were doing and turned toward them, hostile. They were like a stick drawn along among bees—as they traveled they left fury in their wake.

"It must be Boulton," Russ yelled to Burl above the roar of their passage. "He must be charged with the irritating vibration."

Burl nodded as he looked back. The Martians had started after them on foot, and could lope fast when they wanted to. "They've got some sort of organized action going," he called to Haines. "I think it's steam carts!"

"The mass mind caught on fast," said Russ. "And look! They're warned in advance now!"

They were nearing the edge of the city, and looming before them, blocking their right-of-way, were two steam carts—big ones carrying a large number of Martians. They were holding metallic rods and instruments in their hand-members.

Ferrati opened a chest built against the back of the seat and took out a light machine gun. Climbing into the front, next to Haines, he kneeled down behind the windshield, raised the gun, and blazed away.

The steam carts suddenly swerved, one after the other, ran wildly into the side of a building, and turned over. The jeep roared past them, raced across the last hundred feet of city paving and out onto the desert. Haines had to slow down to navigate safely the uneven layers of barren soil, rock and sand. Burl holstered his gun and reached across for one of the abandoned walkie-talkies.

In the excitement of their exit, none had noticed the change in the Martian scenery. But now it occured to Burl that the day was distinctly lighter, and he fancied the Sun—small though it was—felt warmer. The Sun-tap demolished, this was to be expected, and by the same token, radio communication should now be practical.

Sure enough, he got Lockhart's voice at once. Hastily, he warned the commander of what had happened.

As they drew nearer the *Magellan,* the great spaceship lowered toward the ground and let down its grapples and ladders. Burl saw that there was no time to be lost. A stream of Martians and steam carts was pouring out of the city on their trail.

They reached the spaceship and slammed to a halt. The men leaped out. Burl and Russ lifted Boulton's unconscious body from the jeep and, between them, managed to hoist him awkwardly up the dangling rope ladder.

The others hooked grapples onto the jeep, and when it was secure, leaped for safety themselves.

As the first of the Martian steam carts was almost on them, the *Magellan* lifted into the air. It rose high above the surface and swung off into the desert. The Martians drew to a halt. Burl, looking down from the doorway of the cargo hatch, could see them milling aimlessly around. None, he noticed, even glanced up. Air flight, apparently, was an inconceivable phenomenon to them.

After the jeep had been pulled into the cargo hold and secured, the outer ports were sealed. When everyone was safely in the inner sphere, the *Magellan* drew away from Mars and started on the next lap of its long mission.

Boulton was carefully examined. Nothing could be made of his condition. He seemed to bear no physical hurt, although he slept on. He was placed in his bunk, normal, dormant.

The life of the spaceship resumed, for the time being, without him. The next port of call was Jupiter, and that presented problems of its own. Between Mars and Jupiter was the great asteroid belt, a region of many thousands of tiny planetoids, ranging in size from worldlets of two or three hundred miles in diameter down to rocks the size of footballs. "The debris of an exploded planet," was the comment Russ made to Burl. "That's the most likely explanation. Anyway," he added, "there seems to be no Sun-tap station on any of them. The next one is beyond the asteroids, in Jupiter's orbit."

During the next few days, Lockhart and the two astrogators were busy working out a rather complex maneuver, which consisted of having the ship jump over the asteroid belt rather than travel directly through it. While the orbits of thousands of the larger asteroids had been charted, there were thousands more that consisted of just chunks of rock too small to notice. They could not chance a collision with one of these—yet to work out the whereabouts of all of them was impossibly timeconsuming.

What the *Magellan* did was to depart from the plane of the ecliptic, that level around the Sun to which all the planets generally adhere, and to draw outward so as to avoid the path of the asteroids, then to come back in onto the orbit and plane of Jupiter. This involved some tricky work with the various gravitational lines, using Mars and the Sun for repulsion and certain stars for attraction.

There were quite a number of gravity shifts, and during this period no one could be quite sure what his weight would be from one moment to another. There were several periods of zero gravity, when the crew members would float and face the complex annoyances of a steady feeling of free fall. Burl, after a couple of such sessions, got the hang of it rather comfortably.

Lockhart looked at him oddly and smiled. "Glad to know it. I may have a task for you soon, then."

Others found the weightless conditions not so bearable. One of the engineering crew, Detmar, had to be hospitalized. What he had resembled severe seasickness. Oberfield also experienced moments of acute upset.

Boulton's condition did not change. Once or twice he stirred slightly in his sleep, and seemed to murmur something, but then he would lapse back into his coma. Fortunately he did not resist food, and did swallow liquids forced into his mouth.

Except for one or two rare intervals, communication with Earth had ceased. Besides, the mother world was now moving away from them and would pass behind the Sun. Efforts to obtain medical advice for Boulton proved futile.

After they had passed the orbital line of the asteriods and had rearranged their drive so that they were falling freely toward Jupiter, Lockhart called the exploring crew together. "I've got a job for you men," he announced.

Haines, Ferrati, and Burl gathered about the control board to listen. They were restless for something to do —plans for the Jupiter landing could not be made until they knew what the situation was going to be, for it would be one thing if the station were located on that giant planet itself, another if on one of its satellites.

The colonel wasted no time. "While you were on Mars and we were waiting for you, I took the opportunity to examine the outer shell of this ship. You know, of course, that we are constantly being bombarded by cosmic dust, the micrometeorites that always prove troublesome to the Earth satellites and space platforms. The ship has been fortunate in that it has not been struck by any meteoric matter of size, but we have been peppered heavily by dust particles. As a result, the outer shell of our ship is pitted in some spots, and in several places worn perhaps dangerously thin. I don't mean to imply that there are going to be any holes very soon, but I think that there are some parts which we should reinforce or patch."

When he stopped for breath, Burl broke in. "You mean you want us to work on the outer shell?"

Lockhart nodded. "Someone has to do it, and during flights you men are the deck crew. So it's going to be your baby. I am going to keep the ship on free fall for the next several periods and this should make it simpler for you to go outside, in space suits, and do the job."

The next hour saw all three hard at work. Dressed in heavy, sealed, warmed outer-space outfits, wearing metal bowl-like helmets with sealed glass fronts, and drawing oxygen from tanks strapped on their backs, the three men left the inner sphere and emerged on the outer surface of the *Magellan*.

Burl found it a weird and awesome experience. There was no gravitational drag, so that even as he stepped through the exit port, the scene shifted until he seemed to be standing on metal ground, looking upward at thousands and tens of thousands of silent white stars. Nothing moved—except, of course, the space-suited bodies of the two men already half out of sight and looking not quite human. There was no sound save that of his own breath and the faint hum of the radio phone tucked in his helmet.

He was firmly attached to the ship by a long nylon rope which he hooked to rings set on the outer shell. He made his way toward the wide rounded nose of the ship. In one hand he carried a bucket of a liquid plastic resembling tar in thickness and consistency. With a brush in the other hand he would stop—held to the surface by magnetic soles—and smear the plastic protective surfacing over the little pits and pockmarks that now marred the surface of the once spotless ship. The work was not hard, and shortly became a routine which he found did not require much concentration.

It was dip and smear, in a steady rhythmic motion. Haines was working out of sight on a more complex repair job which involved welding a sheet of metal over a badly beaten and sprung section. Ferrati was on the opposite side of the ship.

As he worked, Burl watched the stars, and every now and then was rewarded by the sight of a moving spark of light—an asteroid or meteor. He could see mighty Jupiter ahead—a wide disc of white and yellow, faintly belted with gray and pale blue bands. The famous red spot was not visible. Four of the planet's twelve attendant satellites strung out alongside it, and he recognized them as the big ones discovered by Galileo with his first telescope: Io, Europa, Ganymede, and Callisto. The other eight were tiny, and probably would not be visible until they were right on top of Jupiter, though he supposed that Russell Clyde could probably pick them out now by telescopic sightings.

Burl could hear in his radio the sound of someone whistling softly, and supposed it was Ferrati. There was a short cut-in as Lockhart called a time-shift on the general intercom. A brief exchange followed between Caton in the Zeta-ring chamber of the ship's nose and the colonel, with the information that Caton was coming down into the living section.

Then, after a brief period of silence, Burl heard a series of odd noises on his phones, something went bump, and the sound faded. He was now on the nose of the ship itself, the wide mushrooming surface beneath his feet, and Jupiter high over his head. Bending over, about to smear a dab of plastic on a tiny pitted mark, he suddenly felt himself gripped and pulled.

Caught by surprise, he jerked upward, the brush flying from his hand and sailing into the sky. His shoes clung momentarily to the surface, but their magnetic grip was too weak, and they loosened. He kicked out wildly, falling away into the emptiness of outer space—a space which had a moment ago been a sky and had suddenly turned into a bottomless pit.

He fell backward, seized momentarily by terror. He was brought up short by his rope. It held, and he grabbed it and hung on.

Something had changed. Somebody had altered the ship's drive. The ship was no longer on free fall; it was on gravity drive—and going backward! Not driving toward Jupiter under added acceleration, but fighting to reduce its fall, to stop its drive, to fly away from Jupiter!

In his earphones there was a jumble of sounds. He heard Ferrati yelling and realized that he, too, must be falling away from the ship, saved only by a rope. And the voice of Haines—plastered flat against the surface, the ship driving upward against him.

Vague noises emanated from the control room. Evidently no one was at the commander's mike. He called into it, adding his voice to those of his comrades.

After several agonizing minutes, a voice came over the radio. It was Russell Clyde's and it was excited and angry. "Hold on out there as long as you can! Lockhart's been knocked unconscious! We're trying to get into the engine room and take back control!"

97

Perplexed, Burl shouted, "Who's in the engine room? Take control from whom?"

There was another pause as he heard sounds of pounding, as if someone were trying to hammer open a metal panel. Then Russ's voice came on again. "It's Boulton! He came to suddenly, sneaked up here, knocked out the commander, and climbed up into the Zetaring chamber! Caton was down below—and Boulton's locked the trap door and is running the drive. He's reversed our route, away from Jupiter, and into outer space! Boulton's apparently gone crazy! And we can't get in to stop him!"

Burl, suspended over an abyss, clung to the end of the taut, thin nylon line, as the ship pulled him helplessly along into the uncharted depths of infinity, with a madman at the controls.

CHAPTER THIRTEEN

The Pole of Callisto

BURL SURVEYED his position. Judging from the apparent weight of his body, Boulton was decelerating the ship at a little less than one gravity. The nylon cord was hooked into a bolt near the center of the ship. It would be possible for Burl to climb up it and reach a firmer grip on the outside shell.

There was no time to be lost. An increase in the ship's speed might increase his weight several times over. He began to climb back, reeling in the rope, pulling himself up hand over hand, just as he had done many times in the gymnasium of his high school back home.

Halfway up, Clyde's voice came on his helmet phones. "Will all members of the crew report their present positions to me? Haines?"

He called each man's name, beginning with the three outside. Haines and Ferrati were clinging to the surface, on the far—now forward—end of the ship. The rest of the crew was somewhere in the living sphere. Lockhart was still unconscious. Burl could hear the faint sounds of a discussion in the control room, and also thumps as Caton and Shea continued to try to break open the entry to the generator chambers.

Then Russ spoke again. "Burl, it looks as if you're elected. You seem to be the only one in the right place. There's a hatchway into the nose of the ship from the outside. It's just below the central circle. Can you see it? How close are you to it?"

Burl was almost at the surface now. The circular inset ring that marked the hatchway entry port was a few feet from where his rope was hooked. He described it to Russ.

"Can you reach it without losing your grip? If you

can, do you think you can open it?" came the radio voice quickly.

Burl reached the surface and grasped the hook. He studied the circular panel carefully. "I can reach it all right. There's a holder hook alongside it. But what will I do when I get there?"

"Open it," Russ ordered brusquely. "It unscrews from either side. There's a short lock space between the outer shell and the inner shielding of the generator chamber. Get inside and seal the door after you. From there you can work your way into the emergency nose door to the engines. Keep your suit on. While the generators are shielded, there's no telling what Boulton may have done. The suit will give you some protection.

"After you go through the door, it's up to you. Boulton will be there. You'll have to stop him, somehow. Caton says if you can find the tool kit you may be able to get a wrench to use as a weapon. If you can get through without his seeing you and open the trap door to us, we'll do the rest. But it depends on you."

Burl bit his lip. "Okay. Here I go." There was no question of argument. Everyone's life was at stake, and he happened to be in the strategic position.

He swung over to the panel, hooked his foot under the handgrip and grasped the lever inset in the surface. He twisted it. After a brief moment of resistance, the panel turned slowly. There was a sudden puff as the air within escaped, and then the hatchway stood open. Burl climbed inside.

He caught at the open plug, pulled it back and screwed it tightly from the inside. Now he was in a dark, narrow space. He could feel the flow of air automatically being pumped back in and heard the humming of the generators through his suit.

Working his way along the inner wall in darkness, he finally felt the edge of the metal door that opened into the Zeta-ring chamber itself. He leaned against it, listening, but there was no sound. He turned the handle and threw his shoulder against the door.

It gave, then swung open. He stepped cautiously into the engine room.

It was large and circular, fitting neatly within the nose of the ship. The wide tubes of the A-G generator ring ran around the outside. The reactors were heavy blocks of ceiling-high metal, shielded, and showing only the dials that registered their output. Other machines —the rod storage units and the condensers—were all carefully hidden behind clean metal shielding.

The panel that controlled the engines was unattended in the center of the room. Standing by one of the shielded reactors was Boulton, his back to Burl. He was hammering at the reactor with a bar, evidently trying to tear away the shielding to get at the guts.

Stealthily, the boy made his way to the locker where the tools were kept. Just as he opened it, his hand slipped. The door of the locker clanged against the wall. The burly Marine captain whirled, saw Burl, and gave a yell of rage.

Burl grabbed a wrench and swung it threateningly. Boulton drew back. His face was pale, with an odd expression on it, as if he did not recognize Burl or understand what Burl said. Burl tried to reason with him, but the glaring eyes were those of a total stranger, or, as it seemed then, an alien beast.

Boulton cried in anger, dropped his bar, and charged Burl with his hands outstretched.

Burl swung the wrench, but the strength of the older man tore it from his grasp, hurling it away. The boy tried to dodge, and then the two bodies collided.

The instant the two men touched there was a violent flash of light. Burl felt a shock that left him stunned and reeling. Boulton collapsed in a heap on the floor.

Burl steadied himself, keeping a wary eye on the captain. Boulton sat up slowly, putting a hand to his head. "Boy, that was some kickback," he muttered. He looked at Burl. "Give me a hand up. We've got to get back to the jeep and scram out of here fast. The A-bomb's already set."

Burl was startled. He realized in a moment, though,

101

that Boulton recalled nothing of the past few days—his last memory seemed to be of the blast in the Martian basement. But now, the captain was apparently himself again.

Boulton got shakily to his feet. He seemed confused. "How'd I get here, son?" he asked in surprise.

Burl gave a sigh of relief. "I guess you're all right now. But let's get the trap door to the control room open. Clyde and Caton have got to get the ship back on course. There'll be time to explain afterward."

Half an hour later, when Lockhart had recovered and resumed command, the ship was restored to its proper course. Russ filled Boulton in on what had happened and ventured a guess as to why.

"You must have been given some sort of charge by that globe in the Mars Sun-tap station," Russ said. "It turned you into a sort of robot—a human body running on a charge of alien energy that responded to the commands of the Sun-tap outfit. Apparently, it took a long time before the charge had complete control of your body. Obviously, it then could act only in some general way—telling you to wreck the ship.

"Now, Burl, your body received a charge a long time ago. Whatever its nature, it counteracted or shorted Boulton's when you came into contact."

Both Boulton and Burl thought that made sense. "But," Burl conjectured, "isn't it possible that the charge in my own body has also been shorted?"

Russ shrugged. "Maybe. We'll find out at the next stop. And, incidentally, that's not going to be on Jupiter itself, but on its moon Callisto. We've traced the line of distortions."

"That's good news," said Burl. "I had the feeling you were worried about Jupiter. The planet's so huge it would have meant real trouble trying to land. The books say its atmosphere is thick, unbreathable, and moves in gale velocity around it."

Russ nodded. "With Jupiter almost 89,000 miles in diameter, it would have been a tough problem to maneuver outside this ship . . . in fact, impossible, not to mention the fact that the atmosphere, mostly ammonia and other frigid gases, moves in several independent belts. However, Callisto should be okay."

"That's something we know about our opponents, anyway," said Burl. "They must have physical limitations enough like ours to rule out places where we couldn't move, either."

Boulton showed no further effects from his experience. In time, the *Magellan* drew near Jupiter. Callisto, its fifth satellite outward, moved about the mighty planet at a distance of 1,170,000 miles. It was a large satellite as they go, 3,220 miles in diameter, larger, in fact, than Mercury. But, as Russ explained, it was a queer place in its own fashion.

For despite its size, Callisto was apparently not a solid body as we think of it. Its density totaled only a little more than that of water, its mass half that of the Earth's Moon—a notoriously porous body.

They bore down on Callisto, matching their speed to its, and swung close to its surface. It had almost no atmosphere, just a thin layer of the heavier gases. It was a belted world, without clearly defined continents or surface markings. Its equatorial zone was one vast, featureless belt of darkish-gray. Its temperate zones were white, with patches of yellow here and there. But its poles were gray again.

"The satellite's like a huge ball of thin mud that's never hardened," said Burl as they studied the strange terrain.

"The equator's the softest—it seems to be a river of muddy water, hundreds of miles wide—only it can't be water. Probably semisolidified gases holding dust and grains of matter in suspension," said Russ. "The temperate zones are the same stuff, only colder, and therefore more stable. A thin crust of frozen gases over a planet-wide ocean of semiliquid substance."

"The Sun-tap station's on the southern pole," said Burl. "That must be solid."

It was. The poles of Callisto were actually two continent-sized islands of shell. Dry, mudlike stuff, hard as rock, floating on the endless seas of the semiliquid planet.

The station, a ringed setup quite like the one on Earth, stood in the geographic center of the south pole. The *Magellan* hovered over it while a landing party went down in the four-man rocket plane.

Clyde, Haines and Burl were the landing party. This time, only Burl entered the station after a hole had been blasted in the outer shell. While the redheaded astronomer took samples and made observations, Haines kept watch. Nobody knew what type of defense awaited them here.

Burl found the controls easily enough. He was afraid that he might have lost his physical charge, but it was not so. The controls functioned, the Sun-tap station died. The effect was not very noticeable, for Callisto was already far from the Sun and the thin atmosphere could not diminish the dark sky of outer space. What the great masts caught must have been only the relay from other stations—or perhaps the invisible rays of the distant Sun.

Burl saw no reason to linger, and the three of them gathered up their equipment. As they started back toward the rocket plane, they heard an ominous rumble in the ground.

A sudden spurt of blazing gas shot up from the center of the station. "Duck!" yelled Haines, and they fell flat on the ground. Burl held his hands protectively over his head, as an explosion shook the building.

There was no rain of rocks. Whatever the blast, Callisto's gravity was too weak to attract the debris that flew high above the station.

"It was an atomic explosion!" Haines shouted into his helmet mike. "They mined that station. Run for it!"

They raced for the rocket plane. As they ran, Burl felt the ground quiver beneath him, and huge cracks began to spread, rippling through the hard ground.

They reached the plane and piled in. Russ took off just as the surface cracked open in a thousand places like an ice sheet breaking in an Arctic thaw.

As they rocketed back to the *Magellan*, the whole polar cap, an area hundreds of miles around the Suntap station, split apart. Great spurts of liquid magma, the liquid gas-dust from the heart of the planet, shot up like fountains. Parts of the shell-like polar continent were disappearing beneath this new ocean.

"Their little atomic bomb shattered the thin crust. The whole polar island will probably sink," said Russ. "It was a clever trap. They knew what would happen."

"Saturn next," said Burl. "What'll they have set up there?"

They reached the *Magellan*, loaded the rocket plane aboard, and pulled out, setting their course for the ringed planet. But even as they did so, something was coming from Saturn to meet them.

CHAPTER FOURTEEN

Rockets Away!

THE NEXT lap of their journey was uneventful. Saturn, the next outward planet from the Sun, and the second largest, would present the same problem as Jupiter. This world, famous for its mysterious rings, was about 71,000 miles in diameter and had a large family of satellites—nine in all. The Sun-tap station would be on one of these, Burl thought.

Saturn was also almost as far out from Jupiter as Jupiter itself had been from the Sun. This meant that the trip would be as long for the *Magellan* as the distance they had already traveled to get to Jupiter. Fortunately the A-G drive was a remarkable thing—it was possible to accelerate to fantastic speeds—in theory, probably right up to the speed of light. And so, where great distances were concerned, the ship simply rushed its fall through on Saturn's line of gravitation.

Boulton had fully recovered and showed no lingering signs of the strange electronic charge. Because of the limited size of the crew, Lockhart put the Marine captain back on full duty—he would participate in future landings as if nothing had ever happened.

At the same time, Lockhart cautioned Haines, Burl and Ferrati to keep their eyes on him. It was always possible that the foe's weapon had made some more lasting mark.

Haines had his group make a new inventory of their weapons. Burl, working with them in a space suit, in the partially protected region of the cargo hull, was surprised at the variety. There was a second rocket plane, a two-man outfit. In addition, they had a large store of offensive weapons, including a small but formidable supply of atomic explosives.

Haines gave Burl and Ferrati—who were new to military weapons—brief introductory lectures on their use. Burl saw just what a hand-sized, tactical atomic shell looked like and how it worked. He learned how to operate the heavy-caliber rocket gun which hurled this tiniest of atomic bombs.

And so the time passed, and the amazing disc of Saturn began to grow in their viewplates. It was banded, much like Jupiter, and its brilliant rings surrounded it with a mystic halo that set it apart from all the other worlds of the Sun's family.

Burl was watching Saturn through the largest of the nose viewplates when he thought that he saw a black dot crossing its face. He had located the known moons of Saturn and this was not one of them. Excited, he called Russell Clyde. "Could it be a tenth satellite?" he asked, pointing out the tiny dot.

Russ squinted his eyes; then, calculating mentally, he shook his head, "I don't think so. It looks to me more like something that's in space between us and Saturn. In fact—it must be fairly close to us for us to see it at all." He turned to Lockhart who was at the control panel with Oberfield.

"You'd better have a look. Could be a giant meteor coming in our direction."

"We're moving mighty fast," commented Oberfield. "It should have passed us already if it were a meteor. Instead, it seems to be maintaining the same distance— neither growing larger nor smaller. Acts very odd for a natural body."

"Uh, uh," said Lockhart. "This calls for caution." He quickly went back to the controls, pressed the general alarm button, then called into the intercom. "All hands to emergency stations. Haines and party, please prepare defensive positions."

"This means me," gulped Burl, and scooted down the central hatch, almost colliding with Caton and Shea on their way to the engine room. He met Haines, and, with neat dispatch, all four slipped into space suits. Then out through the cargo hold to posts by escape hatches.

Burl and Haines, at the main entry port, unlimbered the long rocket launcher that had been set up in the passageway. Haines placed three shells of differing strength in position.

They heard through their helmet phones that the mysterious dot was drawing closer. Haines set up one of the launching racks, which was equipped with a telescopic sighter, and peered through the eyepiece. Apparently he caught it, for he grunted, then motioned to Burl to take a look.

It was no natural object. It was the shape of a dumbbell—two spheres joined together by a short middle bar. One sphere was a deep, golden color, the other a bluish-silver, the connecting rod a coppery metal.

"The pattern of spheres certainly suggests the Suntappers to me," said Burl. Haines murmured his agreement.

Lockhart's voice came on the phones. "We've decided it's one of the Sun-tapper ships. We're not going to wait to make sure. Before we left Earth, I can now inform you, I received a directive from the President to regard the builders of these Sun-tap stations as active enemies. My orders are that we are not to attempt to undertake peaceful contact, but are to treat them on sight as armed foes in the field. To do otherwise is to risk Earth's last active defense—this ship.

"I think I don't have to argue this further, considering our recent experiences." His voice hesitated, then rang out firmly, "Haines, you can commence firing at will!"

Haines clicked his tongue and reached for one of the shells. "Okay, Burl, aim at her direct. This one's got a proximity nose that'll beam at her and drive itself wherever she ducks."

He slid the rocket shell into the launcher, Burl sighted, and then Haines pressed the trigger. There was a whoosh of fire and a flare from the launcher's nose. A minute spark winged into the darkness toward the spot, still many miles away, where the strange ship hung.

They watched with bated breath. Suddenly there was

a flash of light from the other ship—a vivid lightning bolt which leaped out and flared up briefly in space. Then darkness again.

"They fired a burst of energy at us. It hit the rocket shell instead," said Haines. "Well, now we know. They use bolts of pure energy—something like the one they fired at Boulton."

He fitted another shell into the launcher, and fired again. Again a spark winged its way, and the bolt of energy burst out to detonate the shell. Burl whistled. "How did they spot it so fast?" he asked.

"I don't think they did. They're firing at us—the rocket shell only happened to be between," snapped Haines.

"Ferrati," he called into his mike, "fire a shrapnel shell at them when I say the word. Advise me when ready!"

Ferrati's voice snapped back. "Right you are, sir. Here it is now, one minute—okay, on target!"

While Ferrati and Boulton were readying their shot from the lower cargo port near the tail of the ship, Haines and Burl had been fitting the largest of their shells into their own launcher. They aimed it carefully at the front-most sphere of the enemy.

"Ferrati, fire!" cred Haines, and then slowly counted to five and pressed the stud of his own launcher.

There was a mementory flicker as Ferrati's rocket shell raced forth below. Then, after a definite time lapse, the exhaust of Haines' heavy shell appeared.

"The shrapnel shell is segmented and doesn't have a proximity guide," Haines explained. "As soon as it's on its way, the nose comes apart into a dozen small shells, each with a standard explosive charge. The shell we used has an atomic bomb warhead and is on proximity guide. It'll chase that ship to the ends of the system if they don't blast it first."

He paused. There was another bolt of raw energy from the dumbbell-shaped craft, and this time a series of flares in the space between—the shrapnel charges had been touched off. Burl held his breath.

"I figure it takes them a while to recharge their gun," said Haines. "Our own blockbuster should get there before they fire again."

Then suddenly there came a sharper flare of brilliant light. For an instant Burl was blinded by the glare. When he recovered, he peered avidly through the telescopic sighter. He saw the ship, but where there had been a golden sphere there was now only a shattered fragment of twisted metal.

The enemy ship changed before his eyes. The remaining silvery sphere glowed brighter, and took on a golden hue. Then it seemed as if the ship were growing smaller. He realized finally that it was retreating.

Burl gave an involuntary shout, and in his earphones he heard the same shouts of triumph from every voice on the ship.

Although it might have been possible to pursue the battered enemy ship, the *Magellan* did not try. They were still on course for Saturn and were not going to deviate.

They reached Saturn after several more days. Matching their great speed with that of the ringed world in its orbit took time, and then they began their survey.

As they had suspected, the Sun-tap station was on one of the moons. The moon was called Iapetus, the third largest of Saturn's family. It was about eight hundred miles in diameter and the next to the farthest satellite from Saturn. Russ was disappointed that they hadn't picked Titan, the biggest moon of all. Titan was over two thousand miles wide and appeared to have an atmosphere of methane.

The view of Saturn was awesome, even from Iapetus' orbit two million miles away. Burl knew it would be a sight unparalleled in the system. The great broad rings, composed of innumerable tiny particles of metal, stone, and possibly ice, encircled it as if held there by an invisible hand. They were, he knew, the particles of a moon that has either come too close to Saturn's great gravitational pull to hold its shape, or else had never escaped far enough to congeal as one solid mass.

Iapetus was a solid world, though. A rocky body, it had a dull gleam, and was streaked here and there with layers of white and yellow, where veins of frozen gases lay forever upon the frigid surface. No atmosphere veiled the surface nor softened the harsh, jagged mountains and clefts of this forbidding little subplanet.

The Sun-tap station stood in plain sight on a high plateau near a polar region. The *Magellan* hovered over it while Lockhart held a council of war.

"I don't see what's to be gained by attempting a landing party," he said. "We've taken all the readings and pictures of the other stations—and we've had a couple of narrow escapes. They've probably mined this one, and they have had plently of time to prepare a trap. I'm in favor of simply dropping an H-bomb on it and leaving."

After a brief discussion, with only perfunctory objections from Clyde and Oberfield who, as astronomers, wanted to land to take other readings, the decision was carried.

The *Magellan* swung up a couple of hundred miles above the Sun-tappers' plateau. Haines and his crew loaded the bulky H-bomb into the main launcher in the tail of the ship. Then the *Magellan* aimed itself at the target, and the rocket-driven bomb roared out.

Down it sped, zeroing in on the wall of the station. There was a blinding flash, a glare as brilliant as that of the Sun itself, as it hit square on the mark. This time Burl watched through carefully shielded viewscreens. The scene was obscured by a wide-flung cloud of white—tens of thousands of cubic feet of satellite rock turned instantaneously into dust particles. After the dust cleared away, they say only a gaping crater where the plateau had been—a volcanic hole, miles wide and glowing red, from which spread vast, deep cracks throughout the entire visible hemisphere of the moon.

The men on the *Magellan* were awed and silent. The thought occurred to each of them, beyond his capacity to deny it: what if this had happened on Earth?

"Of course," said Ferrati slowly, "the low gravity of

112

Iapetus accounts for the greater extent of the disaster. If this had been Bikini or . . ." But under the glares of the rest of the crew, his sentence trailed off weakly.

Lockhart turned away from the viewer. "Mr. Oberfield," he said, unexpectedly formal and official, "you may chart our course for Uranus."

"Aye, aye, sir," said that usually dour personage, with alacrity.

With forced smiles, the rest of the crew drifted away to their duties. The *Magellan* pulled away from Saturn, heading out again toward the limits of the solar system, but it was several days before everyone had quite managed to dismiss the vision of the H-bomb from his mind.

CHAPTER FIFTEEN

Ice Cold on Oberon

NEVERTHELESS, FROM that point on, a different spirit seemed to animate everyone aboard the *Magellan*. There was the feeling that they had closed with the enemy and found themselves not wanting. There was the feeling that they possessed powers not inferior to those of their unknown enemies. The thought had been haunting them all along that they were in the position of a backward people facing an advanced invader—something like the problem of the Aztecs when faced with the gunpowder and armor of the conquistadors.

Now they knew that though the Sun-tappers' weapons were different and indeed advanced beyond Earthly technology, they themselves were not without resources equally deadly to the foe.

After the memory of the H-bomb's powers had been finally absorbed, the crew's activities began to indicate that the ship was coming into the crucial phase of its journey. Haines and Boulton were going over the list of military supplies with sharp, calculating eyes and slight grins at the thought of retribution to come. Ferrati was overhauling the rocket planes and land traveling devices, making them shipshape.

Russell Clyde and Burl surveyed the sky, anxious to be the first to spot what they hoped would be the limping body of the battered and fleeing dumbbell ship, a little atingle at the hope of spotting another such ship —feeling now almost like the hunting dog that has finally spotted the fox.

Lockhart himself reflected this mood of growing excitement. He prowled the ship, examining the mighty purring engines, querying Caton, Shea and Detmar as to how it could better its performance, how fast it could be made to shift speed and directions. He studied the orbits and locations of the remaining planets.

"Uranus is not too far off our path to Pluto," he announced one day. "We'll make it in time to wipe out their plant there. But Neptune, whose orbit is between those of Uranus and Pluto, is away off our track, a third of the way around the Sun. We're going to skip it, hit directly for Pluto and their main base—the end of their line. I don't want to give them too much time to make repairs or to get any reinforcements. I think they're limited in numbers—and we ought to slam them while they still are."

There was no dissent at this. And as the days rolled past, the men of the *Magellan* began to chafe in their repressed desire to finish the matter. At last Uranus came into sight—a large globe, very much like Saturn and Jupiter in that it was of low density and great dimensions. Roughly, sixty-four times the size of Earth, its density was barely above that of water and it probably had no solid surface to speak of. An inhospitable mass of unbreathable gases, at temperatures fantastically lower than the freezing point of water.

As they drew close to the planet, they could see that it also was banded, pale green bands alternating with lighter ones—indicating that some sections of its atmospheric belt moved faster than others. It had five moons which rotated in the opposite direction from those of any other satellite system.

It was on the farthest moon, Oberon, a sphere six hundred miles in diameter, that the Sun-tap station revealed itself. They swung down to observe it and to place their bomb. Not an H-bomb though—they recognized that they had erred in thinking they needed such a powerful explosive.

Oberon was without an atmosphere, a rocky world with streaks of frozen gases, and here and there the sheen of a lake of ice—ice that would never melt—that on this world would be a permanent, hard-as-metal material. There was, nonetheless, something about the surface that seemed to bother Russ.

"Do you notice what seems to be a sort of shifting movement?" he asked Burl. Burl looked, and sure enough, he saw that in places there seemed a flickering of lights.

"Yes," he said, "I see it. What do you suppose it is?"

"I don't know," said Russ, "But I'm going to ask Lockhart to put the ship down and let me take a look."

Lockhart at first demurred, but finally decided that they could afford the brief halt. The *Magellan* approached the surface, safely distant from the Sun-tap station.

Burl and Russ descended in the two-man rocket plane, while the teardrop-shaped ship hung half a mile above them. They landed on a narrow plain, bordered by low ridges of mountains shining with streaks of frozen hydrogen. A layer of cosmic dust hung over the rocks.

Wearing insulated space suits, they left the rocket plane. It was Burl who made the first discovery. He pointed dramatically at the ground. "Look, Russ. This dust is full of streaks and marks. It hasn't been lying here undisturbed. Something has crossed over it!"

Russ kneeled in order to look more carefully. The layer of dust, the consequences of an airless world exposed without protection to the endless fall of cosmic particles, was indeed not the level, undisturbed surface it should have been. Here and there were light, low depressions, as if something had moved across it—like a small snake crawling on its belly. In one place lay a series of depressions, like the footprints of some light-bodied creature.

"Impossible," muttered Russ. "Life can't exist here."

But they trudged on, across the barren flat to a ridge of rock. Here they found what they had thought to be impossible. Clustered along the side of the ridge, in the faint light of the distant and tiny Sun, was a series of thin, blue stalks, about half a foot in height. On each stalk was a flat scalloped top like a little umbrella. It was sometimes bright blue, and sometimes violet. As they drew nearer, these little stalks began to sway, and turned their tops toward them.

"They look like plants," said Burl. "Plants made of something glassy and plastic."

As Russ studied the strange growths, something moved across the dusty tract behind them. It was long and thin and wiggly, with a ridge of tiny crystalline hairs along its back. It was like a snake perhaps, but one made of some unbelievably delicate glasswork.

It slid among the plants and wrapped itself around one. The growth snapped suddenly, and then was absorbed by the creature.

Russ shook his head in amazement. "This is a great discovery," he said incredulously. "This is life! It's life of a chemical type different from the protoplasm of Earth and Mars and Venus. It's life designed to exist among liquid gases and frozen air—life which can't have anything in common with protoplasm. Apparently it couldn't exist even on Saturn's moons—they were too *hot* for it!"

Russ was carried away with the possibilities. "This hints at great things, Burl. Out near Pluto, where the system is even colder, there may be other forms of this frigi-plasmic life, if I may coin a word. This means a whole new science!"

They returned to the ship with their astonishing news. The *Magellan* slowly skimmed over the surface of Oberon. They found whole forests of this glassy frigid vegetation, but not much evidence of any animal life larger than the creature the two explorers had seen.

Over the Sun-tap station—a ringed layout like the others, whose cluster of masts caught the emanations of the distant Sun on the one hand and directed them outward to the still unseen planet Pluto on the other—the ship halted. It drew up fifty miles, pointed its tail and blasted forth a rocket-driven, tactical atomic bomb.

The blast on Oberon was tiny compared to the one which had devastated Iapetus, but it still left a deep indentation in the surface for future space fliers to see.

They left it and the Uranian orbit behind them and

headed outward once again. Behind them now lay the worlds of the Sun's family, while far off to one side lay the tiny light of Neptune. Ahead, between them and the vast gulf of interstellar space, lay only the dark, mysterious ninth planet, the enigmatic world named after the lord of the underworld, Pluto.

The *Magellan* plunged on, in constant acceleration, moving outward to the farthest limit of the solar system. They had traveled almost one billion, eight hundred million miles from the Sun—and yet they still had two billion miles more to go. This was the longest stretch—and during it, they would reach speeds greater than any they had touched before. They shot outward, faster and faster, eating up the infinite emptiness of space, driving the vast stretch that divided Pluto from its neighbors.

The Sun, already small, dwindled steadily. It was still the brightest star in their sky—of all the stars, it alone retained a disclike shape, and the faint flicker of its coronal flames could occasionally be made out—but it no longer dominated the heavens. To find the Sun, they now had to look for it as they would for any other star.

As for Earth, it could not be seen. So close to the tiny Sun it lay that only their sharpest telescopes could bring it out. Even Jupiter showed up only as a thin, tiny crescent near the solar point of light.

"Pluto's a mysterious world," said Burl as he and Russ scanned the heavens for a first glimpse of it. "The accounts in your astronomy books give very little real information on it—but what they give is strange. They say it's the only planet beyond Mars that is a small solid world like the inner ones. It seems to be the same size as Earth—not at all like the big outer worlds. And they say it seems to be the same mass as Earth—a solid world whose surface gravity would be the same as our own planet's."

Russ nodded. "It's an odd one, all right. There's now even some belief that it's not a true planet, but one that was once a satellite of Neptune. Its orbit is pecul-

118

iar; it apparently may cut into that of Neptune. In fact, everything hints at Pluto not being a true child of our Sun. It may be a world captured from afar—a lonely wanderer cast off from some other star, captured by the Sun after millions of years of drifting lightless through space."

Beyond them, in their vision, lay only the stars of outer space, the void that did not belong to our system. And then, finally, they found Pluto—a tiny point of light shining among the blazing stars. They saw the disc, dimly reflected in the light of the far-away Sun.

Even as they were taking their first long look at the dark planet, the general alarm rang. They had caught up with the fleeing wreck of the Sun-tappers' scout cruiser.

CHAPTER SIXTEEN

In Orbit Around Pluto

THERE WAS a mad rush to action stations. Detmar, Ferrati and Oberfield, who had been in their bunks, dashed to their posts while others tried to pass them in both directions. Haines and Burl hastily climbed into their space suits, while Ferrati and Boulton manned the inner defensive controls.

Burl pulled the tight-fitting harness of his insulated space suit over him. The shape of the Sun-tapper ship came into focus on the tiny screen of the air lock viewer. It was approaching them at a frighteningly rapid pace. He could see the broken framework of one of its two globes—the one on which they had scored their hit. The other globe and the connecting passages were strikingly clear. Tiny circles of windows were visible in the passage section, which undoubtedly housed the operators of the vessel. For a fleeting instant he realized that as yet none of the Earthlings had any inkling of what these creatures looked like.

While he knew that the scene was telescopic, the ship was undoubtedly approaching them fast; or rather, they were catching up to it at a perilous pace! Whether the wrecked enemy had slowed down more than they had, as it approached its Plutonian base, or whether some other surprise lay ahead, they had no idea.

Burl felt the jarring impact as Lockhart cut the *Magellan's* drive. There was an instant of weightlessness, and then their weight reversed as the A-G drive strove to slow down the ship. Within the air lock they were outside the living space of the sphere, suspended beneath the drive chamber. Burl could see the walls of the inner sphere whirl past him, a foot away, as the living quarters rotated to shift with the gravitational change. And at that very moment, while all those inside were temporarily helpless, disaster struck.

Burl had just finished adjusting his airtight helmet, and Haines was already on his way forward to the outer shell port and the rocket guns, when there was a flash of lightning from the crippled enemy spaceship. The foe was still capable of fighting—and it had fired first—alarmingly close.

Within what seemed a split second after Burl's eyes had registered the flash on the little viewplate, the *Magellan* received the full force of the mighty electronic discharge. To Burl it seemed as if a thunderclap had sounded in his ears, and as if he had been plunged into a bath of white flames. The walls of the passage sparked brilliantly, blinding light filled the air, and Burl's body vibrated as it would to an electric shock.

He reeled wildly, catching at the walls and almost falling. In a few seconds his senses recovered, although his body was still humming from the blow and his ears were ringing. The viewplate had gone black, the lights in the air lock corridor were dark, and when he tried to gain his feet he realized that the ship now had no gravity; it was falling free without power.

Haines was slumped in the end of the corridor, with the port nearly opened. Burl pushed his way over to him and helped the groggy explorer to his feet. There was no sound, and Burl suddenly remembered that he hadn't taken time to switch on his helmet phone. He did so and was relieved to hear Haines's voice asking if he was all right.

"I'm okay," Burl called. "Let's get this port open. Maybe we can hit back at least once."

Together, they turned the bolts and pushed the thick outer shell door open. Without the aid of telescopic sights they could see the shape of the Sun-tapper vessel plainly, outlined against the curtain of distant stars. Struggling not to think of what might be going on within the *Magellan*—their earphones registered nothing except each other—they unlimbered the long tube of the rocket launcher and aimed point-blank at the foe.

Haines reached into the ammunition locker vault alongside the passageway and selected the biggest and wickedest of the available shells. He twisted the dial in the warhead and, while Burl held the aim, shoved in the rocket shell. With a press of the button, the missile roared out of the tube, racing in an arc of fire directly toward the faint vision of the other ship.

They watched with bated breath, counting the seconds, hoping not to see another blast of electrical fire. But apparently the foe had exhausted its limited resources, for the thin spidery line of rocket sparks reached out, farther and farther, until it seemed to touch the surface of the golden globe.

There was a great flare in the sky now, an outpouring of fire and hot metal. When it cleared away, the sky was empty.

Haines wearily drew the outer port shut. "Now, let's see if we're goners, too," he said quietly. They sealed the outer shell and made their way along the dark passage.

Even as they were unlocking the toggles of the inner hatch, the corridor lights started to flicker. They would light up dimly, and then flicker out, light up again, flare for an instant, then die down. Someone was alive within the ship.

They got the hatch open. In the central section of the living sphere, the lights were also dim and in a few places they were completely out. They emerged and closed the hatch behind them. Only after Haines had tested the inner atmosphere and found it still pressurized, did they open their helmets and climb stiffly out of the space suits, wincing at bruises they had sustained but had not noticed until then.

The air pressure was all right, but there was a smell of burned rubber and insulation in the air. Now that their helmets were off, they could hear voices somewhere above. They found Oberfield lying unconscious, thrown to the floor by the sudden shift of the ship. They climbed into the control room. Lockhart was floating in the air near the open hatchway leading to the engine room overhead. He was calling out orders to someone who was within.

Russ was working over the navigation desk, a bandage around his head, trying to figure out where they would be and where they were heading, without having access to the still dark viewplates.

Lockhart twisted in the weightless air when he saw them. He seemed both relieved and distressed. "I'm glad you're okay, but I had hoped you'd be able to put in a blow for us."

Burl realized that inside the ship they had no way of knowing that vengeance had been served. Hastily, he explained. His word cheered everyone. Russ and Lockhart shouted joyously. Detmar poked his head down the hatch and called the news back to his two fellows who were struggling to get the A-G generators functioning.

The bolt of energy, whatever it may have been designed to do to a ship of the Sun-tapper build, did not have the totally disastrous effect on the *Magellan* that it was intended to have. It had knocked out their electrical system temporarily, burned out some of its parts and caused the A-G system to fail, although the atomic piles were impervious to such currents. Oberfield, Ferrati and Shea were badly hurt.

There now followed an anxious period during which more and more of the electrical system began to function as the men labored to rig up emergency wires, and to replace burned out bulbs and lines. There was a general cheer when the viewplates flickered into life again, though not all functioned. They again had access to the sky about them—even though not all sectors were covered.

The humming in the engine room started up, rose and fell uneasily a couple of times, and then they felt a surge of force. Lockhart fell gently to the floor as the ship began to drive ahead, and then in a few minutes the A-G drive was back on, and the *Magellan* was again under control.

"We took what they had to give, and it wasn't

enough," exulted Haines. "Now wait till we reach their main works. We'll show them!"

Lockhart shook his head wearily as he and Russ worked over the controls. "Let's hope we don't have to show them soon. Our ship is running on emergency rigging. Caton says he's going to have to rest the ship and rewire a good part of the system. Meanwhile, we will be able to reach Pluto safely enough."

Pluto was visible in the forward viewplates. They could see lighter and darker patches on it, almost like the markings of continents and oceans, but there was no evidence of an atmosphere, nor had they expected any.

Readings showed that the average surface temperature was about 200° Fahrenheit below zero, even lower in many places. They searched the surface for signs of their foe.

They found what they wanted on the north polar depression, a basin in the oblate sphere of Pluto. There was no ringed station. There rose a vast pile of dark masonry—a mighty structure covering at least a square mile, a fortress building whose roofs bristled with an array of masts and reflectors. And hanging on patrol over this polar basin were two more of the dumbbell ships.

"We're in no position to come to grips with them," said Lockhart. "I'm going to take the *Magellan* into a low orbit around Pluto's equator. We'll be out of their sight yet near enough to do some probing and exploring while we're making repairs."

This they proceeded to do, swinging the ship down to within a few hundred miles of the Plutonian surface, setting on a fixed orbit around the equator, exactly as the sputniks of years past had first circled the bulk of the Earth. Staying far enough up to maintain orbit, they were close enough to be below the planet's radiation belt.

Taking stock of the ship's condition showed that they dearly needed this delay. Repairs would not be completed for several days. Practically everyone had been bruised or shaken up; Oberfield had a fractured skull and was in serious condition; Ferrati had broken his leg and pelvis; Shea had a couple of cracked ribs. The men were given emergency medical treatment and confined to quarters.

The *Magellan* quietly circled Pluto once every hour and a half and the ship tried to resume its normal life. Russ studied the surface beneath them, Haines and Burl at his elbow. Then, after conferring, the three approached Lockhart.

"We want permission to make a landing," Russ said. "If we take the four-man rocket plane we can make the ground safely. We've got to reconnoiter before we can figure out how to put this master Sun-tap station out of business."

Lockhart agreed. "I was planning as much. Now that we're here, we can't delay just because we're injured. Go ahead."

The three got ready quickly. They donned their space suits, loaded the larger rocket plane with equipment, arms, and plenty of extra fuel. Just before they left, Lockhart gave them a word of caution. "Do not attempt to communicate with the *Magellan* by radio. If Pluto is the Sun-tappers' home world, you may find yourselves surrounded by enemies, and overheard. Don't reveal our existence or position. If you have to talk to us, do not expect a reply unless it's an absolute emergency."

Burl strapped himself into his seat within the rocket plane and glanced through the thick window. Below them was a world the size of Earth—a world which, if it had air and warmth, could most nearly be Earth's twin of all the planets in the system. This rocket plane had touched on the hot surface of Mercury, the first planet. In a little while it would set down on the frigid surface of the last planet. They had come a long way.

CHAPTER SEVENTEEN

Stronghold of the Lost Planet

WITH A jolt that shoved the three men back in their seats, the rocket plane pushed out the cargo hatch, and slid into the dark of space on its own power. Behind them, the metallic surface of the *Magellan* gleamed briefly, and then swung away on its orbit. Riding the red fire of their rockets, they headed on a long low dive for the mysterious surface below.

Pluto was a vast hemisphere, half lighted in the faint, dim glow of the tiny Sun, half in the total darkness of outer space. Here and there wound a silent, frozen river of glistening white. They passed over a gulf of some frigid sea of liquid gases, from which islands of subzero rock projected, and moved inland over a continent of lifeless grays and blacks. Haines gently drew the ship lower and lower, and at last the rocket plane bumped to the ground.

It rolled a few yards and stopped. The three men crowded to the door, tightened their face plates, and forced open the exit. There was a rush of air as the ship exhausted its atmosphere. Then, one by one, they stepped onto the bleak surface of the Sun's farthest planet.

"I feel peculiar," whispered Burl. "This planet reminds me of something."

"I have the feeling I've been here before," Russ said slowly.

Burl felt an odd chill. "Yes, that's it"

Haines grumbled. "I know what you mean. I can make a guess. We've never really been the right weight since we left Earth. Even under acceleration there were differences one way or the other. But I feel now exactly as I did on Earth. That's what gives you the odd sensation of return."

The two younger men realized Haines was right. For the first time since they had left their home world, they were on a planet whose gravity was normal to them. It felt good and yet it felt—in these fearful surroundings —disconcerting.

Above them was the familiar black, unyielding sky of outer space. No breath of air moved. Yet somehow the scene resembled Earth. "It's like a black-and-white photo of a Terrestrial landscape," said Burl.

There was a field, some hills, a tiny frozen creek and the dark shapes of rounded mountains in the distance. All without color except for the cold, faint glow of the star that was the Sun.

A thin layer of cosmic dust lay over the surface, such as would be found on any airless world. Russ scooped beneath it and came up with a hard chip.

He squeezed it between his gauntleted fingers. It cracked and broke into powder. He whistled softly. "You know what this feels and looks like" he said as they came close to the frozen creek on the little hillside. "It feels like dirt—common, Earthly dirt. Like soil. And you know what . . . I can already tell you one of Pluto's secrets."

They stopped at the creek. It was a layer of frozen crystalline gases. Haines pushed the alpenstock he was carrying into it and scraped away the gas crystals. "I think I can guess," he said, "and I'll bet there is ice under this gas."

"Pluto was once a warm world with a thick atmosphere," said Russ. "Notice the rounded hills and the worn away peaks of the mountains. Those are old mountains—weather-beaten. This hill is round—weather-beaten. This creek, those rivers of frozen gas—they follow beds that could only be made by real rivers of warm water. The soil that lies beneath this dust—it could only happen on a world that knew night and day, warmth and light, and rain and wind. Pluto was once a living world, a place we'd have called homelike."

Burl shivered a bit. "Out here? So far from the Sun? How and when?"

Russ shrugged. "We'll find that out. But the evidence is unmistakable." They walked on.

There was a low, cracked wall on the other side of the hill, and beyond the wall stood the roofless ruins of a stone house, silent and gray in the airless scene.

They waited with surprise and uncertainty. Haines drew his compressed air pistol, but there was no movement. The scene remained dead and still—the windows of the house were dark.

They advanced on it and flashed a light inside. It was an empty shell. There was no glass within the wide and low window openings, and no door.

"They went in and out the windows," commented Burl, ducking through one of the openings. "And they weren't built like us."

"No," said Russ, "there's no reason to suppose the inhabitants would have been built like human beings."

Inside there was nothing to see, and they left. Beyond, they found a straight depression in the ground filled with flat swirls of cosmic dust. "This looks like a road," said Haines.

They returned to the rocket plane in order to follow the dead roadway more easily. Passing between the low, dark cliffs of rocky mountains, they came to a plain marked by thousands of columns of rock, pieces of crumbling walls, and many straight depressions that must have been streets. It was the remains of a world that had died.

They found, as they traveled northward and made intermittent landings, that there had been many cities. Now all lay in ruins. There had been great roadways, now covered with the debris of outer space. There had been mighty forests, now miles of petrified black stumps. It was a gloomy sight.

In their landings, they had found inscriptions on walls and bas-reliefs carved on mountains. They knew from these what the Plutonians had looked like, and they had a suspicion of what had happened.

The Plutonians had been vaguely like men and vaguely like spiders. They had stood upright on four thin, wide-spread legs and had two short arms. Their bodies were wide and squat, and they seemed to have been mammalian and probably warm-blooded. They breathed air out of flat, thin nostrils and their heads joined their bodies without necks. Two oval eyes were set below a jutting bald brow. They had worn clothes, they had driven vehicles, they had flown planes.

Their vehicles had globe-shaped power plants. Their airplanes had globes where wings should have been. Their cities and their engines—which existed now only on wall pictures that were probably once advertisements —were built along globe-and-rod principles.

"There's no doubt," said Russ, "that the Sun-tapper culture and the Plutonian culture are the same. It's the descendants of the Plutonians that we are fighting."

"But how could they have survived?" Burl asked. "This world was never part of the solar system when it was warm."

"We'll soon know," said Russ. "Tomorrow we're going to see how far we can get into their polar redoubt. Somehow we've got to blow up that last station."

"And I think we three are going to do it," said Haines. "The *Magellan* will never take the place from the sky. We'll have to do it from the ground."

Now they were reminded of Earth again. For the first time since they had departed from the United States, night fell. They had not been on any other planet long enough for such an experience. But the effect here on Pluto was mild.

Day was like a bright, moonlight night. Night then meant that the dim Sun had set and, in effect, it merely made the landscape slightly darker.

They compared notes late into the night in the rocket plane. By dawn, when again the dim glow shone, they had come to some very definite conclusions about the planet.

A number of the drawings on the walls seemed to have some religious significance. They focused on the phases of a moon. There were symbolic representations of this moon, passing through its phases; presmuably

Plutonian religious and social practices were related to it.

"But where is this moon?" Burl had asked.

"I think," Russ answered, "that what some astronomers had suspected about Pluto was right. It did not originate in the solar system, but was captured from outer space. Originally it revolved around another sun, some star which was light-years away. How it tore loose from that star we'll probably never know—the star might have simply become too dim, their planet might have been on a shaky orbit, an experiment of theirs might have jarred it loose, many things could have happened.

"Once beyond the gravitational grip of its parent sun, the planet wandered through the darkness of interstellar space until it came within the influence of our own Sun. How long this took would again be a guess. Possibly not more than a few thousand years, I'd say, since somehow a remnant of the population managed to survive. This suggests that they had some warning. Enough time passed for them to build the big structure we noticed at the north pole, probably to store food, build underground greenhouses and make sealed homes for a few families. Inside this giant building the last of the Plutonian people kept going.

"Then came the moment when their planet fell into an orbit around our Sun. I'd guess they emerged to find that the new Sun was too far away ever to heat up Pluto again, or to permit the rebuilding of an atmosphere. So they worked out a new scheme. This was to blow up the sun into a nova—make it a giant and thereby bring its heat all the way out to Pluto—warming this world again, lighting it again, unfreezing its gases and waters. So they set up the Sun-tap stations."

"That also accounts," added Haines, "for their limited number of spaceships and their need for secret operations."

"Yes," said Burl, "but there are two things that don't fit in. What happened to their moon—surely it would have gone along with Pluto since it revolved around it?

130

And second, why the thirty-year delay between the first Sun-tap stations and the completion and operation of them?"

There was no answer to these questions yet. The three began the morning's expedition.

As they neared the pole, they stayed close to the surface, for, any moment, they expected to see the dumbbell ships that patrolled the sky above it.

At last they set down the rocket plane on the edge of the polar plateau and got out. Not more than a mile away, the black ramparts of the building—a wall running miles across the horizon—rose hundreds of feet into the sky.

Above it, they caught a flicker from the forests of masts and the glint from a dumbbell ship. They moved silently forward carrying the rocket launcher on their backs and a small load of shells and several hand bombs. These made heavy baggage, but the distance was not far, and the purpose great.

Burl felt like an ant about to creep into a human house. But he reflected that no ant ever had such dangerous intentions. An ant enters a house to steal a crumb of food. But if an ant had intelligence and evil intentions, it could cripple such a house.

Such was the situation for the three of them as they neared the precipitous walls. On arrival, they found that entry would be easier than they expected.

The Plutonian refuge had not been built to offset attack from the surface of the planet itself. It was no thick rampart of unbroken plastic as the walls of the other Sun-tap stations had been. Close up, it proved to have many doorless entryways, ramps running up to higher floors, even wiry monorail scaffolding, probably left behind by the builders.

They entered an opening in the base. Once inside, dim lights set in the ceiling lighted the path before them. They walked down this culvert like rats in a giant sewer until they came to a wall studded with several doors.

The doors were shut, but a tiny globe set on the surface of each one reacted to Burl's charged touch. Two opened upon dark airless passages. The third resisted a moment, and when it did open, there was a whoosh of air which raised a momentary cloud of dust on the stone floor of the culvert. This was obviously the entrance to the inhabited portion of the refuge.

The men closed the door behind them. They were in a small chamber. A door on the other side was opening automatically. "An air lock system," muttered Russ as they went through.

They were now inside the vast building itself. There was air, and, after testing it, they opened their helmets. The air was almost as thick as that of Earth, and they experienced no difficulty in breathing. It was stale and somewhat metallic in flavor, probably because it had been enclosed and used over and over for thousands of years.

They saw no living beings, which seemed strange. "Apparently these people really are at their last gasp," remarked Russ as they passed through an area that had obviously once been a large dormitory. They heard distant humming sounds somewhere in the floors above, but all that was visible on the lower level seemed to be maintenance machinery.

They walked through great storerooms which were piled high with healed drums. They saw factories lying silent—curious lots of odd machines powered by globes that were idle. They skirted an unlighted reservoir of water in a circular chamber far in the interior. And here and there in the gloom, they spotted huge ramps leading spirally upward.

Finally they turned their steps up a sloping ramp, mounting one floor and then another, and another. They were tired, but curiously exhilarated. They felt that they were about to strike at the heart of the foe, and that his days were numbered at last.

They emerged on a higher level, lighted more brightly than the others. Here they saw globes that glowed with the same intensity as those in the Sun-tap stations had. They moved carefully now, keeping out of sight, and several times they saw shadows in the distance or heard the thump of something moving.

They worked their way by instinct to what they guessed was the center of operations. They peered, at last, through a low, wide doorway into a large chamber. Here was a mass of mighty globes and rods, some revolving as they circled the metals masts that came through the room from the ceiling above.

"It must be the base of the Sun-tap receiver line," whispered Haines. "This should be a good enough place to set up our time bomb."

They stole over to a cluster of globes and unpacked the powerful little atomic bomb they had carried with them. They carefully put it together, inserted the explosive fuse, and set the timer. "I'm giving it four hours," said Haines. "Time for us to get out of here and radio the *Magellan* to get into action. That should take care of this station."

They moved carefully out again, scarcely breathing for fear of some Plutonian entering and discovering them. They made their exit safely enough and started to retrace their steps.

Back down through corridors and strange chambers they moved, stopping every little while as something that sounded like footsteps passed over them. "Where," Burl whispered, suddenly troubled, "is the stolen heat and power of the Sun going? It isn't heating up Pluto. Surely they can't simply store it."

"Something we haven't solved," Russ replied hurriedly. "From what I remember of the masts, it looked as if they were relaying it somewhere else again."

"Can't imagine where," said Haines. "Not back into space, surely?"

They fell silent, concentrating all their energies on not losing the way. "Are you sure we came through here?" Burl asked nervously. "I don't remember this at all."

"I don't, either," said Russ. "It looks queer. Are you sure we're on the right path?" He turned to Haines.

The explorer shook his head. "We must have made a wrong turn. I think we've lost our direction."

They hastily conferred, and decided the best thing to do was to make their way to the lowest level and then outward—but suddenly they realized they could not tell which way was outward. There were no windows, and the wall markings and direction signs were unintelligible.

To make matters worse, they heard new noises, and, just as they dodged into a corner, five Plutonians shambled through.

These creatures were as the ancient wall sculptures had depicted them, though a bit smaller than their ancestors. They were pale, almost white in skin color, and their eyes were tiny sparks of red. They wore light harnesses around their bodies, and two of them were carrying tools. They spoke together in clacking bass voices. They shuffled loosely over the ground on their four thin legs. Burl thought of them as ugly caricatures of semi-humans.

When the creatures had passed, the three explorers darted out to where a ramp spiraled to the lower levels. They started down in single file, but it was too late.

Staring directly at them were two Plutonians who had come up from below. The men pushed past, but not before a barking voice had cracked out an order.

The Earthmen started to run down, followed by the scrabbling sounds of their pursuers. The barking calls increased in volume.

From somewhere a booming sound began, repeated over and over. As the men emerged on the floor below, they heard it repeated on every level. "The alarm's out for us," called Haines, making no effort to keep his voice down. "We've got to run for it!"

Laden with the remaining weapons and equipment, the three human beings hurried on, but it soon became clear that four legs were better than two, for the creatures were gaining on them.

They had forgotten they were lost. Now they sought only to get out of sight and hide. They dropped their equipment as they ran down halls, through tunnels, skittering along sloping ramps, heading for what they hoped would prove to be an exit.

Behind them an increasing crowd of Plutonians had collected, and several times a spark of electronic power crackled and blazed against the wall over their heads. The pursuers were armed.

Burl's lungs began to ache painfully. Close on the heels of his companions he dashed into one room only to find a group of Plutonians coming at him from the other side. His ears were deafened by the barking noises and alarm boomings. He jumped to one side to avoid a Plutonian standing directly in his path, and ran into a narrow tunnel. There was an excited barking as the creatures followed him.

With a sinking heart, he realized that he was now alone. Haines and Russ must have been cut off. He gasped for breath. Running in a tight space suit, carrying his oxygen tanks, was hot and hard work. He did not dare drop the tanks, for his only chance was to escape outside.

He ran wildly on, hoping to reach an outer door. But he seemed now to be in a maze, for nothing was familiar to him. He could no longer remember how many times he had run into groups of Plutonians, nor could he guess how many followed on his heels.

Then he stumbled into a small, round chamber out of which led three tunnels. As he looked around quickly to select his next means of escape, barking Plutonians erupted from each opening. Burl backed up against the wall, knowing that this time he was trapped.

A blaze of sparks broke over his head as a blast banged across the room. The red-eyed, scrabbling figures charged, their chinless mouths opening to emit barking calls of bestial anger. One aimed a rodlike contrivance at him, and there was another flare of light.

The room dissolved around him in a glare of brilliant

green. As he slipped helplessly to the floor, he lost consciousness.

CHAPTER EIGHTEEN

Sacrifice on the Sacred Moon

BURL DENNING! Can you hear me, Burl Denning?" A thin, tinny voice somewhere was calling him. But the darkness was all around, and Burl felt a great sleepiness and a desire only to sink deeper into the cottony nothing in which he seemed to be cradled.

"Burl Denning! If you can hear me, speak up!" Again the faint, scratchy voice nagged at Burl's mind. He really ought to answer. He tried to open his mouth. Something hard and cold was pressing against his back. He tossed and squirmed.

Once more the voice called, and this time he decided that he must be asleep. He struggled to open his eyes, then finally blinked them wide in an effort to adjust himself to his surroundings.

He was apparently out in the open, and it was night. The sky was dark, not black, but almost so—a deep, blue-black. There was a pale blue saucer hanging in the sky. It blotted out most of the view. Gradually, he became aware of a shiny barrier between him and that sky—he was not out of doors. Something like a glass dome seemed to be overhead.

Burl raised his head. There was no one in sight. He felt dizzy and confused. He lifted a hand to his brow, and felt the cold glass of his space helmet. He was still wearing his space suit then. The voice—it must be in his helmet phone.

"Hello," he ventured weakly. "Who's calling?"

Quickly the faint voice replied, growing stronger. "Burl, are you all right? Where are you?"

Burl looked around. He was sitting on the floor of an isolated enclosure with a transparent dome. There were no walls, just the rounded dome like a fishbowl turned upside down on him. The flooring beneath his feet was plastic.

"I'm all right, I think," said Burl. "Is that you, Russ? Sounds a little like you, but you must be far away."

"Yes, it's me, Russell Clyde," confirmed the voice. "You're coming in weak, too. Where are you?"

Burl described his surroundings. There was a silence for a moment, then Russ's voice again. "I kind of suspected it, but what you say confirms it. We must be on the only planet we haven't visited . . . or rather, not on it, but near it. I mean Neptune. I knew from the gravity I wasn't on Pluto any more. Judging from our weight, and your description of the bluish planet in the sky, we must be on Triton, Neptune's bigger moon."

Burl found that his dizziness was disappearing. "I feel light," he commented, as he got to his feet. "Should Neptune look sort of like Uranus, only more bluish in color?" he asked.

"That's it," said Russ. "Neptune is pretty much of a twin for Uranus, only it's denser, a little bit smaller, and perhaps more substantial than the other giant worlds in our system. It should have a second moon, smaller and way out."

Burl walked around the little enclosed space. "I guess I'm a prisoner here," he said. "This dome is on the surface. Most of the area is just a sort of rocky plain with patches of liquid gases, but there are a couple of big buildings nearby. Funny sort of structures— they have fancy tops with symbols on them that look like the phases of the moon."

"I think I'm inside one of those buildings," Russ guessed. "I'm in a big hall with a lot of exhibits in glass cases. And they've got the strangest creatures I've ever seen in them. There are lunar markings here, too— they remind me of the ones we saw on Pluto. You know what I suspect?"

Burl paced around, regaining his senses as he walked. It was obvious that, after he'd been knocked out by the Plutonians, he had been taken by them to this moon of Neptune. For what purpose?

Russ continued to murmur his thoughts, his voice ringing tinnily in Burl's earphones. "I think that Triton was originally Pluto's moon. When Pluto wandered into the solar system, it crossed Neptune's orbit and was held. Its moon came closer to Neptune and was captured completely. But Pluto, having a greater mass, didn't stick. It established an eccentric orbit of its own which took it far out from Neptune for hundreds of years at a stretch and brought it back only rarely. Pluto lost its moon. And that moon was the spiritual home of the Sun-tappers' religion."

Burl glanced across the landscape. There were some funny things growing nearby. They looked a little like thin, glassy trees with big, blue coconuts on top.

"What happened to you and Haines after we got separated?" he asked, still talking through his helmet phone.

"I don't know what happened to Haines," said Russ. "I hope he got away. But they trapped me. I was taken aboard one of their dumbell ships, and brought here. The trip took days. I guess you were unconscious for all that time. If it's any comfort to you, the Pluto building was destroyed. Our atomic bomb went off. I saw the flare from a window in the ship. I think this moon is the last stronghold of the Sun-tappers, and I think it is our final objective."

The strange crystalline vegetation seemed to be moving closer to Burl. He watched it carefully. It *was* moving! There were living beings out there!

They glided oddly over the ground, and he saw that their bases were a mass of crystalline fringes, moving feelers which crawled over the surface bearing the upper structures with them. They had thin, trunklike bodies with two long, pencil-like branches that were used as arms. And the coconut objects were heads!

They circled the dome now, and Burl could see that each round blue knob had a central black spot that apparently served as an eye. There was no sign of nostrils or mouth. Burl stared at the creatures in wonder.

The beings were clearly gesturing to him, trying to signal with their odd arms. He waved back, wondering how he could establish communication. As he did so, he described the creatures to Russ.

Russ's voice was excited. "Say! I think I've figured out what sort of place I'm in. This is a museum of galactic life! Each of these glass cases contains a specimen of the highest form of life of its particular world. In one of the cases, opposite me, there's one of the Martian creatures—a big, antlike fellow. He's standing there, looking perfectly alive, but absolutely motionless. Next to him is something else that looks like an intelligent form. It's sort of a man, covered with short red hair. Around its waist it's got a belt. and there are pouches on it, and something like a short sword. It must be a humanoid type from some world out among the stars. Some of the others look like intelligent forms, too, because they are wearing clothing.

"I think that collecting these specimens and setting them up here is part of the religion of the Sun-tappers."

While Russ was talking, Burl thought of a way he might communicate with the stick-men. He wanted to draw a diagram of the solar system on the floor of his enclosure. He gestured futilely with his hand, but there was nothing with which to make a marking. The stick-men outside watched his hand, then one of them reached around to something hanging across its back and withdrew a thin table and a wedge of red. Holding the table up to that Burl could see, the creature quickly sketched a recognizable map of the Sun and its planets!

Burl realized then that he was dealing with highly intelligent beings—no savages, these, but the products of a high civilization. He indicated the third world as his own. The stick-man drew back as if surprised, then pointed upward.

They came from Neptune!

During the next few hours, a most curious three-way

discussion went on—Burl signaling to the Neptunians outside and describing his discoveries to Russ over the phone of his space suit; Russ suggesting answers to some of the more difficult diagrams. It was a curious experience. Gradually, by means of simple drawings and gestures, and even charadelike playlets acted out by the weird vegetable-crystal beings, there emerged the general story of the Neptunians and the invaders from Pluto.

On Neptune there had been a great civilization covering the entire world, a hard surface lying deep beneath its thick methane atmosphere. There were forests and there were animals and intelligent beings. They did not breathe, but absorbed both their food and liquid gas through rootlike feelers on which they stood and moved.

Then one day, about thirty years ago, they had been invaded by creatures that came in dumbbell-shaped spaceships, and which had destroyed their cities, and attempted to conquer the planet. They learned that these ships had come from Triton, the strange new moon that Neptune had acquired about a thousand years earlier, and from the new planet, Pluto, their astronomers had observed at that time.

For thirty years the Neptunians had fought against the invaders. For a while they almost succeeded, but then something new had developed. Their world grew hotter. Great structures had been erected on the poles, the areas first conquered by the Plutonians and still held by them. For these spots, vast amounts of heat surged over the planet and changed it.

Heat meant death and doom to every living frigiplasmic thing on Neptune. Desperately, they increased their warfare, but the heat sapped their strength, destroying them, until now they knew it was but a matter of time before the Neptunians, beast and vegetable alike, would vanish totally.

"So that's it," breathed Burl. "That's where the Suntap energy is going. The Plutonians want Neptune because it's near their old moon, and they have to warm it up to live on it. Of course! And Neptune's too far from the Sun to explode when it novas, it will just get comfortable for the Plutonians!"

The Neptunians continued their strange tale. They had built a crude spaceship and manned it with a suicide battalion of the most desperate warriors of their race. They had journeyed to Triton in hopes of seizing it and destroying the foe from there. The stick-men had attacked and had been beaten back.

Now there were only a few dozen of them left—the last soldiers of their invasion and ignored by the enemy. And here they were, explaining this to Burl, whom they recognized as an ally.

Russ's voice suddenly broke into Burl's thoughts, "There's some sort of ceremony beginning here. There's a procession of Plutonians dressed in golden robes marching down the center of the hall, carrying staffs with moon pictures on them . . . They're chanting in unison, though it sounds like barking. Can you hear it?"

Burl could. It sounded faintly in his earphones like the noises in a dog pound.

"Now they're circling around. They're opening one of the cases. The glass slides back . . . Say! The exhibits aren't dead. I see something moving . . . It's a man!"

Russ's voice stopped suddenly. Faintly, Burl could hear the barking and then Russ's terrified voice. "It *is* a man, Burl. He's dark-skinned and wearing white cotton pants and a homespun shirt. He looks like an Indian, maybe a South American Indian. When they lifted the glass, he just walked out and stood as if he were all mixed up. Then he got scared and started to run."

The voice was silent a moment. "They grabbed him, Burl. They *sacrificed* him! And now they're coming for me."

"Stop them!" Burl yelled wildly. "Do something!"

"I can't stop them." Russ was resigned. "They're taking me to the empty glass case. I guess I'm elected to be the next exhibit. They're shoving me in!"

Outside Burl's enclosure the stick-men sensed something unusual in his strained attitude. They stared in at him, while he remained tense, listening.

Now Russ's voice came again. "They're going to take off my helmet and throw in the suspended animation gas, Burl. Good-by. I can see them still. Oh . . . oh, I feel strange, I feel stiff, faint . . . here . . . I . . . go. . . ."

His voice faded out, thin and weak. Then there was only silence.

Burl threw himself against the restraining transparent wall of his dome prison and hammered on it with his fists. The dome would not give way.

He looked around desperately, determined to escape, wondering what surprise the Plutonians were holding him for—suspecting he would be the next victim. They would be coming for him soon, he knew.

He searched the enclosure for some way of leaving. He looked at the stick-men and wondered if they knew. One of them, the one who seemed to be the leader, gestured to him. His arm pointed to a spot in the floor.

Sure enough, there was a crack there, an outline like a small trap cover. He worked at it with his fingers and, finding a dent, he pushed. A lid came off. Below was a cleared space, a few inches deep, in which were set the levers of a typical Plutonian control board.

Burl wondered if he were still carrying the charge that attuned him to such controls. The shock he had received on Pluto could have blanked it out.

He pushed at the levers with his gloved hands. They did not obey him. Desperately, he removed the glove from one of his hands. It was bitter cold in the little enclosure. but there was some atmosphere. The lever almost froze to his fingers, but he turned it again.

This time it worked. The top of the dome that entrapped him suddenly opened, and the sides slid back. Burl replaced his glove on his hand and dashed outside to the freedom of the frigid surface of Triton.

Then he was among the Neptunian stick-men, and they were actually patting him on the back, waving toward the building, hurrying him on.

They were prepared to die in one last desperate assault on the foe. Could Burl do less?

CHAPTER NINETEEN

The Museum of Galactic Life

THERE WERE a number of structures laid out on the plain under the blue glow of Neptune. Burl saw that only one of them was a true building in the design he had come to know was that of an ancient Plutonian temple except that it was far, far larger than any of the ruined shells he had seen on Pluto.

The other structures turned out to be walls and pillars arranged around the central building, evidently in relation to their religious significance. This main building, ornately decorated, was windowless, and the several closed doors represented metallic and forbidding barriers. It must have covered thirty acres, rising about thirty feet from the ground.

As Burl frantically examined it, the leaders of the Neptunians moved discreetly with him. They gestured at the doors, indicating their own inability to open them. Apparently they though that Burl might succeed where they had failed.

Burl wasn't sure he could. He supposed there might be controls similar to those that released him from the dome, but he thought first he had better determine a plan of action. Somewhere within, Russ was sealed up —an exhibit among the living dead of many planets.

He managed to convey this thought to the three stickmen. There was an unmistakable nod of assent from one of them; and a twiglike arm indicated that Burl should follow him. They rapidly crossed the area to the outlying fringers of a frigi-plasmic forest.

Here towering crystalline masses pushed up from the dark ground. It seemed to be a weird jumble of broken glass—broken glass ten and fifteen feet high! The Neptunians led Burl into this amazing landscape through a narrow path. He walked behind them, feeling thick and heavy in comparison with their fragile bodies. But, in spite of appearances, they were not fragile, nor were the growths that made up the fantastic Neptune-transplanted vegetation of Triton.

They came to a clearing amid the forest of blue and green and orange crystals, and there were the rest of the Neptunian survivors. Burl counted about forty, rooted in pools of liquid gas, absorbing renewed energy while waiting for commands. As he entered the clearing, most of them lifted their root tentacles and crowded around him. He was as strange a being to them—helmeted and bundled in plastic and rubber and metal—as they seemed to him.

Burl noticed that many of them must have been wounded—there were signs of missing arms or of burned roots, and few had odd poultices smeared over their round, blue heads.

The Neptunian commander pointed out their store of arms. They had long spears of some glistening translucent substance, a projector which fired darts of the same material, and a number of the Plutonian globe-and-rod instruments—obviously captured from the enemy.

He examined some of the spears and darts, and a suspicion he had held on first seeing them was confirmed. These were made of ice! On Neptune, ice was easily obtained—and hard enough to be worked like metal. Its melting point being far, far above any heat likely outside of a Neptunian laboratory, it was as permanent as iron for their needs!

Burl studied the captured Plutonian hand weapons, and was pleased to have one of the Neptunian soldiers pick up one and demonstrate how it was fired. It had apparently simpler controls than most Plutonian products, for it easily blazed forth a bolt of electronic fire that blasted a tall, crystalline tree to shards.

The Neptunian leader began to gesture again, and conveyed to Burl that they wanted to attack as soon as possible. He gathered that conditions on Triton were not the best for these people—that their ability to hold out was limited and that they desired to make their final assault without delay. They wanted to know now what Burl could contribute.

Burl realized that as far as he was concerned, he was not in any better shape than his allies. His oxygen tanks were slowly but surely emptying. He examined his gauges and was startled to see he had only two more hours before suffocation would set in. The suit was warmed by batteries which would last several days longer, but by that time it would be too late.

Somewhere inside his suit he had a pocket knife, but he could not get at it in the frigid near-airlessness of the outer surface. His holster still rung at his side, but it was empty.

There was nothing to do then but to join the Neptunian assault. He would try to open the door by the electronic charge that still remained in his body. If he did, they could break in and do what they could. If he could not, who knew what would happen?

Burl picked up one of the Plutonian weapons and gestured to the rest to prepare to attack. Immediately, they fell into orderly ranks. They were, indeed, soldiers, Burl thought—the cream of their planet's armies— whatever that meant in Terrestrial terms.

Then, following the lead of the Neptunian captain, they marched out of the forest. As they crossed the open plain, Burl knew that they were probably in sight of the defenders. But he realized quickly that that had been true when he was released and nothing had happened. So perhaps he was wrong. Perhaps the Plutonians were limited—perhaps they had not bothered to keep a watch.

That left only the Plutonian spaceships to worry about. Burl hastily searched the sky and located two glowing spots—four really—undoubtedly two of the double-sphere ships. The Neptunians behind bumped into him, then the whole column came to a halt.

Burl pointed to the ships. The commander waved his arms helplessly. They had been there all along, Burl gathered, and what could he do about it? More gestures. Yes, the ships were dangerous. In fact, they had been the ones that had defeated the main Neptunian attack, blasted them from the sky and destroyed the ship in which the stick-man army had arrived. The Neptunians were going to attack, regardless.

Again, Burl realized the essentially suicidal mood that moved these beings. They were attacking against odds before which they were utterly helpless.

Even as Burl stared at the far-off lights of the Plutonian ships, he noticed them swing away, moving off toward the horizon. As he watched, he thought for an instant that something else had blinked like a star, far in the distance.

Struck by a sudden thought, he activated his helmet radio. "Burl Denning calling the *Magellan!*" He spoke at maximum power into his throat mike. "Calling the *Magellan!* If you can hear me, reply!"

Then, to his joy, a faint, faraway voice answered, "Burl Denning! This is Lockhart. Give us your location."

"Lockhart! There are two Pluto ships approaching you from the direction in which you can hear my voice. Be careful!"

The voice came faintly again, "We see them. We'll take care of them. Haines made it back to the ship. The Pluto base is destroyed. There are only those two ships left. We followed them here as fast as we could. Can you hold out until we draw them out and crack them? We will need a little time.

Burl called, "Don't worry about me. Go to it. Russ may be alive in their building here. Don't bomb it. I'm going to try to get in."

"Okay," called Lockhart's voice, already growing weak as the *Magellan* and the two pursuing foes drew away.

Burl turned to the Neptunian captain. He drew his hand across the sky to show that the ships had gone, drawn away from their protection of the temple. He pointed at the walls of the building with a "let's go" gesture.

Burl noticed that though the Neptunians were apparently featureless, he could sense a distinct tightening up in their actions. They were tensed, ready for the final battle.

They marched up to the main door of the temple. The captain loosed a bolt of electronic fire at it, but it left no mark.

There was no sound from within. Evidently the Plutonians were either busy about their own business, or did not regard the Neptunians as worth their attention.

In a covered panel right next to the door, Burl found the typical Sun-tap controls. He tried to work them, but they would not function through his gloves.

He hesitated, knowing that removing his glove this time might prove very risky. Then he hastily drew off his left gauntlet and the thin nylon glove that was the inner protection of his suit. He placed his hand on the control. The icy cold bit into it. He twisted, the control worked, and he tore his hand away, replacing the gloves.

The door slid open. Burl ran inside, followed by half a dozen Neptunians. They were in a small antechamber, evidently an air lock.

The Neptunians, leaping with excitement, did not bother to activate the inner door, which would have meant closing the outer door. Instead, they attacked it with heavy ice axes. The strange tools, chilled to a hardness unthinkable on Earth, bit into the fragile plastic. After a few hard blows, the plastic split, and there was a small explosion as the air within the temple burst through. A gale of escaping gases roared through the little chamber, ripping the rest of the door to shards and hurling the Neptunians right and left. Outside, the flow began to congeal, and a thin snow of liquid air began to fall.

When the blast subsided after several minutes, the Neptunians jumped up, shook off the new gas-snow, and charged through the doorway into the temple itself.

Burl held his Plutonian flashgun at the ready. Inside, they found chaos and disaster. In the great rooms and halls Plutonians writhed on the floors, in the last throes

149

of suffocation and freezing, now that the air had been ripped from their stronghold.

The walls bore brilliant paintings and sharply defined sculptures. Advancing with the ranks of stick-men, Burl caught glimpses of strange scenes on distant planets, of landscapes that must have been Pluto at one time, beneath a double sun that probably was its original parent.

Burl became faintly aware of a distant clanging. Not all the air was gone, he thought; it must be pouring out in slower volume as the pressure diminished. Somewhere an alarm was ringing.

The Neptunians fell behind; he saw now that the floor and walls of the temple were still too hot for them. They began to withdraw, regrouping, blazing away with ice darts and spears at Plutonians who had appeared in hastily-donned space garments.

Burl fired, then plunged on. He had to get to the hall where Russ was imprisoned.

Finally he was out of sight and sound of the Neptunians and their adversaries. Behind him a door swung down. He was nearing the heart of the building now. The remaining Plutonians were sealing it off, rallying for their final defense.

He was now cut off from support. But he still counted on confusion and surprise to aid him. He ran down a long hall to a vast central chamber and arrived a split second before the door slammed shut after him. The museum of galactic life!

It was a huge hall, oval in shape. In its center was a block that might be an altar. Lining the walls on each side, ranging from the great door on the far end to the equally ornate one through which Burl had come, were floor-to-ceiling niches with gently curved, transparent fronts. He could see dark shapes standing motionless within each of these exhibition cases.

There were also about two dozen Plutonians in the hall, most of them grouped around the central altar. They wore gaudy harnesses and carried sharp, sword-like wands.

Two of them started for Burl, and he leveled his

weapon and fired. There was a flash of light and one of the creatures dropped senseless. The other turned and scuttled away, uttering barking cries.

Burl glanced hastily around. The rest of the Plutonians—priests or curators or executioners, whatever they were—advanced slowly on Burl. He couldn't get them all, but he'd try. He fired it again.

This time the weapon failed to go off. Its charge was used up. The Plutonians yelped with delight and pressed forward, flourishing their swords.

Burl desperately hurled a globe-and-rod at them, meanwhile looking around for a new weapon. But he saw only the shining glass fronts of the exhibits. In the nearest case was a manlike being, dark purple in color, a thing with a fixed but intelligent stare in its slanted yellow eyes. It had two tall ears, a wide chest, and a curling tail, and was wearing a belt with pouches and a short kilt that only about half covered his two long, hairy legs.

Burl spun on his heel, swooped upon the gleaming swordlike wand that had fallen from the dead Plutonian, and racing back to the exhibit, brought it up with all his might against the transparent surface.

The glassy stuff cracked. Another blow with all the strength of an Earth-muscled body on a light gravity world, and the front shattered open.

There was a puff of a greenish gas. The creature inside suddenly blinked and moved a hand. Then, without waiting, Burl dashed to the next exhibit and swung his metal sword again.

The barking calls of the Plutonians increased in frenzy, and they charged him, screaming. As the second exhibit crashed open, Burl turned to fend off his attackers, swinging his sword. It clashed against the sword of the nearest curator-priest, who slipped and went bowling over against his fellows. Burl reached the third exhibit and smashed it.

He turned to meet a renewed attack, and this time, out of the corner of his eye, he saw that a purple humanoid was in action beside him. The purple one had picked up a Plutonian, apparently with great ease, and was using its body as a bludgeon.

Something furry and green leaped high in the air and came down in the middle of the Plutonians. There was a wild, unearthly screech as it landed, and exhibit number two, from heaven knew what starry world, was in the fray.

Now Burl found himself momentarily unhampered, and rapidly he opened exhibit after exhibit. The battle became wilder and fiercer, as star-being after star-being joined in.

The Plutonians swung away in all directions with their wands. Their barking voices were drowned out by a rising chorus of sounds—roaring, inhuman voices, calling curses in languages of worlds that lay many light-years distant—wild, birdlike calls from a winged being whose intelligent eyes and wide brow belied the ferocity of its beaked and taloned attack. There was a clanking, ringing sound, as a thing of half jointed shining metal, half soft, velvety-white flesh, whirred among the foe, doing damage with a razor-edged arm that shot out from the metallic part of its body.

There was something like a cloud of insects—a mad thing which seemed to be a single hive of tiny winged cells that moved and bit and stood its ground like a single united being.

There was a Martian that had at first stood stupidly, as if unaware of what was going on, and then had gone berserk at the first sight of a Plutonian running past him.

And in the next case was Russ, still space-suited, staring out through the glass. With a joyous crash, Burl smashed the front of the niche.

Russ moved, his eyes opening wide as he saw Burl. He reached down quickly and picked up the helmet which had been taken from his head. As soon as he had it in place, he activated the phones. "Wow!" his voice came in Burl's earphones loud and clear, "Let's go!"

He jumped down and grabbed Burl. Together, the

two danced a wild jig of joy. Then they both remembered the Plutonians and turned, realizing that they had momentarily left themselves wide open to attack.

But there was nothing to be afraid of. The Plutonians were all torn, beaten, lifeless. Moving among them were their former victims—the exhibits gathered from worlds undreamed of by human astronomers. What hopes of vengeance had been stored in those inhuman hearts when each had been torn from his native world, had been caught in helpless paralysis and carried trillions of miles across trackless space as living trophies!

Although their forms were many and strange, there seemed to be no fear of one another among the survivors. What they had been through had united them forever. One by one, they began to gather around Burl and Russ, recognizing in them their saviors, grateful for their delivery.

Burl's helmet radio spoke up. "The *Magellan* calling Burl Denning! We have eliminated the last two enemy ships. Give us your location. We intend to A-bomb the installations on Triton as soon as we can pick you up!"

Burl spoke into the phone. "Hold up the explosions, colonel. We've taken the place intact. You can land the *Magellan* outside the main temple and come and see. We've got allies, lots of them."

"Yes," said Russ into his phone, "we've got the secret of Pluto, we've got a friendly, fellow world on Neptune, and we have a whole crowd of the strangest refugees you'll ever hope to see. Bring extra space suits with you. We have the markings here of friendship and trade with dozens of distant star planets—a treasure in itself worth a dozen trips around the solar system."

Burl looked around him, thoughtful at these words. Visions of the marvels that future A-G ships would find, as, manned by Earthly crews and carrying each star-being back to its galactic world, they opened up on each planet new vistas of achievement, science, and artistic marvel.

He found himself staring into the yellow eyes of the big, purple humanoid. His hand was grasped by the

153

other's strangely shaped hand while a yellow, powdery creature like a human moth tried to touch Burl in fondness.

Burl smiled widely and began to grasp the proffered tentacles, pincers and grippers.

"Welcome," he said to them all. "Welcome to the solar system. We've got a lot to talk about."

About the Author

Donald A. Wollheim was bitten early by the science-fiction bug. As a boy, he filled many thick notebooks and scrapbooks with clippings, pictures, and facts about the planets, and astronomy in general.

He grew up in New York, graduating from New York University, and at once began a successful career as a free-lance writer of science fiction. Since 1946 he has been editor of a publishing house specializing in paperback books. A number of anthologies of the fantastic are the result of his editing.

Aware of the widspread interest in this subject, Mr. Wollheim decided to inaugurate science fiction conventions, and founded the Fantasy Amateur Press Association as well. He considers himself a true science fiction pioneer.

Among his hobbies are model soldiers. He is considered an authority on them and has a fabulous collection.

If you enjoyed SECRET OF THE NINTH PLANET you will
want to read these Science-Fiction Best Sellers
from Paperback Library

ALL THE COLORS OF DARKNESS

by Lloyd Biggle, Jr.

The chilling adventures of one man's struggle to conquer—
or be conquered by—Time! "Weird adventure, well-told,
for science-fiction fans." (Library Journal)

52-514, 50¢

BEYOND THE SEALED WORLD

by Rena Vale

A masterpiece to rank with CHILDHOOD'S END and
GREEN HILLS OF EARTH—a strange adventure of an
outcast struggling for survival in a warp of time.

52-811, 50¢

INVASION OF THE ROBOTS

edited and with an introduction by Roger Elwood

Science-fiction at its exciting best! Daring and dangerous adventures by eight great science-fiction writers: Isaac Asimov, Henry Kuttner, Jack Williamson, Richard Matheson, Philip K. Dick, Robert Bloch, Lester Del Rey and Eric Frank Russell.

52-519, 50¢

ALIEN WORLDS

edited by Roger Elwood

Ten startling science-fiction adventures by Poul Anderson, Robert Bloch, John Brunner, John Campbell, Philip K. Dick, Edmond Hamilton, Eric Frank Russell, Robert Sheckley, Clifford D. Simak and John Wyndham.

52-320, 50¢

EARTHMAN, GO HOME!

by Harlan Ellison

Science-fiction adventures into the terror and danger of infinity—16 excursions into the far-out zone where the incredible meets the impossible and the earthman meets the cosmic creatures.

52-508, 50¢

CONTACT

edited by Noel Keyes

Man faces extra-terrestrial life in exciting tales by the masters of science-fiction: Ray Bradbury, Fredric Brown, Harry Walton, Fritz Leiber, Robert Sheckley, Peter Phillips, Murray Leinster, Howard Fast, Ian Williamson, Clifford D. Simak, Howard Koch and Isaac Asimov.

52-837, 50¢

ADAM LINK—ROBOT

by Eando Binder

Adam Link—the first of the robot race—had photo-electric eyes, an iridium-sponge brain and the soul of a man! Since Eando Binder first wrote about him, Adam Link—Robot has become one of the most famous characters in science-fiction. Now, for the first time in paperback, here is a novel incorporating the startling adventures of Adam Link—a robot battling for existence in a world that misunderstands him, fears him and exploits him.

52-847, 50¢

BEYOND THE BLACK ENIGMA

by Bart Somers

Commander Craig faces a hideous death as he attempts to save the world by rocketing beyond the Black Enigma.

A Commander Craig Galactic Adventure.

52-848, 50¢

THE WORLDS OF SCIENCE FICTION

edited and with an introduction by Robert P. Mills

"The best in science-fiction today." (Detroit News) "Glitters like a Who's Who is science-fiction and fantasy." (Buffalo News) An anthology of s-f stories by today's masters: Asimov, Bradbury, Sturgeon, Heinlein, Blish, Boucher, Collier, Bester, Davidson, Fast, Knight, Elliott, Van Doren, Anderson, Cassill and Miller, Jr.

"A COLLECTION TO MAKE THE S-F READER PROUD OF HIS TASTE, AND TO LEAD THE GENERAL READER TO WONDER WHAT OTHER WEALTH HE'S MISSED." (Fort Wayne News Sentinel)

54-819, 75¢

If you are unable to obtain these books from your local dealer, they may be ordered directly from the publisher

PAPERBACK LIBRARY, INC.
Department B
260 Park Avenue South
New York, N.Y. 10010

Please send me the following books:
I am enclosing payment plus 10¢ per copy to cover postage and handling

Book # .... TITLE .... No. of copies ....
    # .... TITLE .... No. of copies ....
Name ....
Address ....
    ....